Corner Kick

Corner Kick

Bill Swan

James Lorimer & Company Ltd., Publishers
Toronto

James Lorimer & Company Ltd. acknowledges the support of the Ontario Arts Council. We acknowledge the support of the Government of Canada through the Book Publishing Industry Development Program (BPIDP) for our publishing activities. We acknowledge the support of the Canada Council for the Arts for our publishing program. We acknowledge the support of the Government of Ontario through the Ontario Media Development Corporation's Ontario Book Initiative.

Cover illustration: Steven Murray

The Canada Council | Le Conseil des Arts
for the Arts | du Canada

ONTARIO ARTS COUNCIL
CONSEIL DES ARTS DE L'ONTARIO

National Library of Canada Cataloguing in Publication

Swan, Bill, 1939–
    Corner kick / written by Bill Swan.

(Sports stories ; 66)
ISBN 1-55028-817-2 (bound).   ISBN 1-55028-816-4 (pbk.)

I. Title. II. Series: Sports stories (Toronto, Ont.); 66.

PS8587.W338C67 2004   jC813'.54   C2004-900476-X

James Lorimer & Company Ltd.,   Distributed in the United States by:
Publishers   Orca Book Publishers
35 Britain Street   P.O. Box 468
Toronto, Ontario   Custer, WA USA
M5A 1R7   98240-0468
www.lorimer.ca

Printed and bound in Canada.

Contents

To Jenny and Jon
who played soccer;

Duncan
who is starting to;

and
Jack and Justin
who prefer hockey.

Our game is fair play.

1

Soccer Season Begins

Michael Strike could see fear in the goalie's eyes.

The soccer ball was close to Michael's feet, under his control. Nobody could take him now. He shuffled to the left, deking the lone defender out of position. He caught the rolling ball with the inside of his right foot and shifted back to the right.

The fullback tripped trying to reverse direction. Michael dribbled into the clear, with only six metres and one frightened goalie between him and the goal.

"Let 'er go, Mike!" yelled Brandon, his right wing forward. "Bulge that twine!"

Michael edged forward, keeping the ball close to his feet. Bulging the twine would be a good trick. They were playing on the bare hard-packed earth of the school playground. The metal frame of the goal was regulation size, but had no netting. Bulging the twine, as Brandon urged, would be impossible. Michael smiled at the thought.

The goalie froze for a moment. Instead of moving forward to cut the angle and make it harder to get the ball past her, she retreated. She stumbled half a step backward, stopped to look left and right to find the goal posts, and retreated one more step until she stood on the goal line. Or where the goal line would have been had one been marked.

"Boot it, Strike!" Brandon yelled again.

Michael smirked, ragged the ball from foot to foot, and shuffled forward. He brought his right foot down hard on the edge of the ball. The ball bobbed up from the ground, rising almost knee high. Michael brought his right foot around, winding up for a heavy kick.

The goalie winced once and stumbled backwards, covering her face. Michael faked the kick, then brought his foot back into position before gently tipping the ball over the goal line with the little toe of his right foot.

"All right!" said Brandon, pumping his fist to the sky.

"You all right, Erika?" asked Michael. The goalie got to her feet. She brushed dirt from her jeans.

"I thought you were going to drill it at me!" she said.

Michael laughed. "Somebody would have had to chase the ball. That would waste good practice time. I wouldn't want to wear the team out."

"And you might not have scored," said Brandon. "You might have hit Erika by accident. Boy, did she look scared!"

Erika brushed at her shirt sleeves. "Okay, Mr. Smart Guy, you stand here and let Michael drill one at you. We'll see how many you'll catch and how brave your front teeth are."

Brandon said nothing.

Miriah Bushra rushed up from midfield. "So what is this? Are we all going to stand around and admire the superstar?" Miriah had shoulder-length brown hair, green eyes that sparkled, and nerve that even Michael envied.

"Fetch the ball," Michael replied. The ball had rolled only a couple of metres past the goal.

"Fetch yourself, Fido," Miriah replied. "You're a team member like everybody else, not visiting royalty."

"Yeah, but he's the best bet we have of winning a soccer

game this year, here at Tarcisio Parisotto Elementary School," replied Brandon. He pronounced the school name with some exaggeration: "Tar-Chees-yo Par-i-zot-oh El-e-men-tar-ee."

"Game? We're after the championship this year," said Erika.

Miriah shook her head so her hair cascaded from side to side. "As long as Mr. SuperStar doesn't strain himself," she said. "We wouldn't want to ruin his soccer season for something as silly as a championship."

"If I thought I'd get hurt playing with this bunch," Michael said, mainly to Miriah, "then I wouldn't be here. I wouldn t risk my whole soccer season for any *school*."

From the middle of the field, Ms. Wright blew a long, shrill blast on her whistle. This was the signal for everyone to gather in the centre of the field. The practice was about to begin.

Michael excelled at everything. He wore the coolest clothes, watched the best movies, played only the most recent games — if a new version came out, his mother was first in line to buy it. He did as well in school as he wanted to do, which was high B's. High enough to satisfy parents and teachers, and not so high that other kids resented him. He was popular in school. His Grade Seven classmates were suitably impressed when his father drove up to pick him up one day in his brand new, bright yellow Hummer, a vehicle large enough to push a school bus.

But to Michael's surprise, what really caught Miriah Bushra's attention was soccer. One day that spring his picture had appeared in the local newspaper. He had scored the winning goal to help the Oshawa Kicks indoor soccer team win the provincial championship.

He had been popular before. Now he was a school hero. When tryouts for the school soccer team were announced, his classmates asked him to play, and Miriah's voice was loudest.

Michael was reluctant at first, but Miriah had persisted. She had gazed at him without blinking, her eyes such a vivid green everyone mistakenly thought she wore contact lenses, and said, "Michael, the team needs you."

She paused, still unblinking, and said, "The school needs you."

Miriah had never before paid any attention to Michael. If he was a hockey hero, Miriah would not likely have noticed. She had loudly proclaimed to the class one day that she thought hockey to be a brutal, sluggish game fit for Neanderthals. She told someone later (who told someone who told someone until everyone knew) that she said it to deflate Kyle McIntyre, whose crush on Miriah at the time was as well known as his love of hockey.

Miriah had a world vision. She preferred European bands, foreign movies that no one could understand, and, of all things, ballet, mainly because her parents hated it. Someone once told her that soccer was the world's most popular game, so she became a soccer fan.

"Are you playing?" he had asked Miriah.

"But I … don't…" She blushed and dropped her eyes. Michael had never seen her flustered before.

"We could be teammates then."

Miriah gave him a funny glance, followed by a faint smile. But that afternoon she and Michael were both part of the eleven — exactly the number needed for the team — to turn out for soccer practice. The May air was still chilly, and the line of maple trees around the schoolyard had not yet added their leaves to the green patchwork of the Oshawa spring.

"Thanks for coming," Ms. Wright said when the group had ceased most of their shuffling. "We're going to have a lot of fun this year." They were a mixed group: some Grade Sixes, mostly Seven and Eights, although two energetic fifth graders bounced on the spot.

Soccer goals sat at either end of the hard-packed dirt field behind the portables. One side of the field ran downhill to a baseball diamond in the park next door.

"Can we win some games, too?" asked Erika, shaking her ponytail. "Last year we had lots of fun but we got creamed a lot."

"Yeah, who enjoys that?" Kyle added. He had red hair that kept falling over his eyes.

"Well, last year was our first year with a team," said Ms. Wright. "And my first year as a coach. We all learned a lot. We'll do better this year."

Brandon Sales, with his short, dark-brown hair and perfect smile, bounced a soccer ball off his foot. "Well, this year we got Mike Strike playing for us. Mike'll eat up those other teams. He plays on the Oshawa Kicks."

"We all know that," said Miriah, her voice haughty.

"It's Michael," Michael said firmly.

"He'll cream everybody," said Justin Little, one of the Grade Five students. "Nobody can stop him!"

There were nods and grumbles of agreement, enough that Michael started to blush.

"All right, all right, everybody," said Ms. Wright. "That's enough. We're glad to have Michael on the team this year. Welcome, Michael."

"Provincial champions," said Brandon. "Mike's team won the Kingston tourney, the Kitchener tourney, the Windsor tourney, the …"

"We get the idea," said Miriah, scornfully. "He's a superstar."

"And the indoor league championship this past winter, and a whole bunch of indoor tourneys, and …"

"Okay, enough," said Miriah. "What are you, his press agent? Cheesh."

"If you can do it, it's not boasting," replied Brandon. "And Mike's done it."

Michael turned to Brandon. "It's Michael," he said, again, quietly.

On the first day of school that September, Mr. Rahilly — who was new to the school — called him Mike. He disliked the name. When he had tried to correct the teacher, his voice had squeaked out a mouse-like "Michael" and the class had laughed. He had never been laughed at before, and he did not want to be laughed at ever again.

"Thank you, Brandon. That's quite enough," said Ms. Wright. She turned her coach's eyes to the clipboard she cradled in her left arm. "I have your names now. Michael, Miriah, Erika, Brandon … " She read off the list of players, her voice almost drowned in the May breeze. "… Justin, Alysha, Kyle, and Victoria."

The breeze swept the names away. In the short pause that followed, Michael ran his eyes along the pattern of brickwork on the school wall, each brick lapping the one above and below. He was fascinated by the way things like the bricks fit together to create something no one could imagine when looking at a single brick.

"Soccer is a team sport," said Ms. Wright. "That means every one of you must do the job you are assigned. That job will depend on the position you play."

"Yeah, yeah, yeah," mumbled Brandon.

"You have something to say, Brandon?" asked Ms. Wright.

"No. Well, yeah. You say this every year."

"Brandon, this is only the second year I've coached the soccer team. If I said this last year, too, maybe it's because this is important."

A few players giggled. Brandon scowled.

"Now listen, all of you. This is important and I'm only going to say it once." The players quieted. Even Justin stopped bouncing.

"This is co-ed soccer — the boys and girls play together. Because Parisotto Elementary is small, we can field only one team. You'll be playing against schools with an entire team of Intermediates."

"What's that?" asked Justin.

"Players older and bigger than you, Squirt," said Kyle, who was almost two metres tall.

"Intermediates are Grade Seven and Eights," said the coach. "We don't have enough students to field a team of Intermediates. In fact, we just have enough players for one team with nothing to spare. So if we're going to play soccer, we need every one of you."

"Like me," said Justin. His short blond hair was flipped back at the front. His blue eyes sparkled as though he had just done something he should not have.

Erika adjusted her sweatband.

"Is that why the school board is going to close the school?" she asked. "My parents say this is the last year."

All the chatter suddenly stopped. Ms. Wright looked one at a time at each of the students. They all stared at the ground.

"Enrollment at this school is small," she said. "And yes, the school board has included Tarcisio Parisotto Elementary on a list of schools to be considered for closing."

"That means they're going to close us," said Erika.

"No decision has been made," said Ms. Wright. "And it's not going to have anything to do with soccer season. We have only six weeks until school's out. The first game is next week."

"Next week?" Alysha said.

"Yes, next week. After the league games, the top four teams

go into the playoffs. The winners of the first round play for the district championship."

"But if they close our school we'll have to go to Pines next year."

"That's not our worry now. Soccer, Erika. Think soccer. We don't have time to make mistakes. The only way to make sure we're going to the playoffs is to win games."

Michael listened. He felt anger filling his head until he was sure he looked like a blowfish. The board couldn't do that, could they? Make him start a new school in Grade Eight? His parents would straighten that out, he was sure.

"We got creamed a lot last year," said Erika. "Because we're a small school."

"You've said that, Erika," said Ms. Wright. "And we're still a small school. But I want every one of you to think of winning."

"Make it to the playoffs," added Miriah, as if voicing a strange concept.

"That's right." Ms. Wright paused for a moment. "One more thing is just as important," she said.

"More important than winning?" asked Erika.

"Just this. I want each of you to repeat this three times. Are you ready?"

The team members exchanged glances and nodded to Ms. Wright.

"Repeat this: 'My game is fair play.' Three times. Ready?" She waved her hands as though conducting a choir: "My game is fair play. My game is fair play. My game is fair play."

"So what's it mean?" Ms. Wright asked Justin.

The small boy beamed. "We don't kick the ball out of bounds. We keep it in fair."

"That's baseball, Twerp," said Kyle.

Victoria gave Kyle's arm a playful cuff. "It means we play fair with the other team and with each other," she said. She was dressed in a denim jacket and jeans with a green grass stain on the knee.

"Yeah, right," Michael whispered, mostly to himself.

"And then we win the championship," said Brandon.

"Yeah, Smarty, how do we do that?" asked Erika.

"We just give the ball to Michael and let him score," said Brandon, laughing loudly at his own joke.

"Some team," said Miriah.

"Not yet," said Ms. Wright. "But it will be. Everyone will have an opportunity to play. Everyone must play. And where the team needs you is more important than the position you like to play."

"Centre forward," said Michael emphatically.

"Right forward," said Brandon.

"Goal," said Erika.

"We'll determine that as we go along," said Ms. Wright. "As coach, I will decide who plays what position, and who goes on the field and when. No back talk. Are we clear?"

Brandon mumbled.

"Okay. Everybody on the goal line. Roll out all the balls. Right. For this drill, I want to see everybody down the field and back again. There are ... how many? Eleven? We have six soccer balls. So what's that going to mean?"

"We share?" asked Victoria.

"You got it. Ready?"

The spring air was pierced by the shrill whistle. The team set off, kicking the soccer balls ahead, passing, shouting, dribbling. Down the field and back again they ran, arriving at the goal line where they started, some panting, all laughing. No one was surprised that Michael was the only one without a partner and that he finished first.

"That was good," said Ms. Wright. "Now do it again. Kyle, can you work with Justin for a bit?"

"Do I have to? I mean, why do we have to have these little kids on the team? They can't do anything right."

"Kyle, Justin needs some help on taking a pass. Your assignment is to help him. We don't have any bench strength, so we need everybody."

"Do I have to? Me and Brandon ..."

"Don't whine. Just do it."

School soccer season had begun.

2

Miriah's Fundraiser

When Michael heard footsteps in the school lobby a week later, he wasn't really intending to sell tickets to anything.

"That was a great game Monday night against Pines," Miriah said, as she came up behind him. She held a green file folder in her hand. A few Grade Two students worked on a giant mural, fitting photographs into a pattern on the wall. Through the gym door they could hear sounds of a bouncing basketball and the squeak of sneakers on hardwood. On the gymnasium stage were the tables and boards that the chess club used for their noon-hour games.

"Well, yeah, it was okay," Michael replied.

Two nights before Tarcisio Parisotto Elementary had won the first game 3–0 over Pines Elementary. Michael had scored all three goals.

"It almost wasn't fair," Miriah said. "You had the ball most of the game."

She was right. Michael had used his dribbling skills to keep control of the ball and move it from end to end. Only when he had tried to pass had Pines taken possession. So, for most of the game he had dribbled the ball, confident that no one could take it away from him.

"Thanks," said Michael.

He moved toward the door to the school playground. Miriah followed him.

"Want your tickets now?" she asked.

Michael turned. "Tickets? What tickets?"

"War Orphans of the World," said Miriah. "Remember?"

"Oh, yeah," said Michael. "War orphans." When Miriah had made the presentation to class, he had volunteered to help because everyone else did. But now that he thought of actually selling tickets, he realized he hated selling anything.

Brandon banged his way through the playground door and came toward them, a soccer ball in his hands.

"War orphans?" he said. "Miriah, you're always trying to save the world. Why don't you give it a rest?" He turned to Michael. "You comin'?"

"Be right there."

"Brandon," said Miriah to the back of Brandon's head. "I need you, too. Don't go."

"What?" said Brandon, turning around.

"I took a whole load of old clothes down to the Salvation Army," said Michael. "Isn't that enough?"

"You did?" asked Miriah.

"Well, my Mom did. Same thing," Michael said, ignoring Brandon. "Yeah. She's on this kick about sharing our good fortune with others."

"Sounds familiar," said Brandon.

"I bet that old Blue Jays jacket was the first thing to go," snickered Brandon.

Miriah opened her folder. "The old clothes usually go to poor people who live here, not war orphans," she said. She handed a booklet of tickets to Michael and another to Brandon "Here are your raffle tickets."

"Tickets?" asked Brandon, starting to clue in. "Am I supposed to sell these?"

"War orphans, remember? The class agreed to sell raffle tickets to raise money to help kids in Bosnia and Rwanda and Afghanistan and Iraq and other places all over the world. I printed them up on my computer. Then I cut them up and stapled them into these booklets. Ten tickets to a booklet."

"They're stapled real good," said Brandon.

"How much?" asked Michael.

"Fifty cents a ticket."

"But—" said Brandon.

"You don't have to learn to spell Afghanistan," said Miriah. "Just sell tickets."

"What's the prize again?" asked Brandon. "People are going to want to know that."

Miriah placed the backs of her wrists on her hips. "Sometimes I think you don't listen at all," she said. "Blue Jays tickets, remember? My Dad got them."

"Blue Jays tickets?" said Brandon. "Wow!"

"Yeah, wow."

Michael fanned the book of tickets in his hand. "What if we can't sell them?"

"What? You don't think you can do it? Is that it?"

"No, I can do it. It's just …" Michael wasn't sure.

"That's what Alysha said."

"Alysha? Do you think she'll sell any? Even I can do better than her," Brandon boasted. "We both could."

"You sure? Alysha took two booklets," said Miriah. "She figures she'll sell more than anybody in the class."

Brandon reached out. "Gimme three," he said. "I can sell three booklets, easy. Three for Michael, too."

When Miriah thrust three booklets into his hands, Michael looked at them and wondered how he had got volunteered. Even for Kicks fundraisers he avoided selling stuff.

"Is it true they're closing the school?" Michael asked, wanting to talk about anything but the thirty — thirty! — tickets he had to sell. "That would be cruddy."

Brandon shrugged. "My folks say its about time. The school's old and falling apart."

"But we'd have to go …"

"To Pines, yeah," said Brandon. "Wouldn't that be neat? They have a big gym, and coaches and lots of good stuff."

"Coaches didn't help their soccer team much," said Miriah.

"And a big playground. And school dances."

"Well, my parents," said Miriah, lifting on her toes as her voice rose, "say we've got to do something about it."

"Here we go again," said Brandon. "Miriah to the rescue."

From the stage, three chess pieces flew through the air, bouncing down the steps and landing at their feet: a Queen, a King, and a Rook.

"Things are getting a little rough in the chess club," said Michael.

"Miriah, think of all those little orphan pawns," said Brandon, slipping his ticket books into the rear pocket of his jeans.

Mr. Cachuk, their math and science teacher, came down the steps. "Down here, Jason," he called, pointing to the chess pieces. "Now pick them up."

A boy who looked to be in Grade Six shuffled down the six steps. With a sidelong glance at Mr. Cachuk, he picked up the pieces and retreated.

"It's too bad you're not still coming out for chess," Mr. Cachuk said to Michael.

"Give someone else a chance," Michael replied. *Fat chance*, he thought. In the fall he had joined the chess club. He had thought he was good, but soon found others were just as good. He liked to be the best.

"Besides, who knows, you might have beaten me," said Mr. Cachuk.

Michael laughed. One club player in the eighth grade had beaten Mr. Cachuk that spring, and his picture had been on the local TV news and in the newspaper. But by then Michael had quit going out for chess.

"Well, your help would have been useful this year," said Mr. Cachuk. "These young ones, sometimes I wonder …" Mr. Cachuk had difficulty controlling his class's behaviour.

"It must be nice to be so talented, Michael," said Miriah. "Like a superhero."

"Oh, that wasn't *too* sarcastic," said Brandon. "Come on, Michael. Let's go."

"Well, any time you want to come and help out," said Mr. Cachuk, retreating up the steps to the stage. "We could use you, Michael." Two kids on the stage began arguing and another chess piece flew.

"Yeah," said Michael. As an afterthought he called after the teacher. "Say, Mr. Cachuk, would you like to buy a ticket?"

"Raffle for War Orphans? Sorry, Alysha beat you to it."

"Come on!" said Brandon. "The bell goes in fifteen minutes. Let's go out and bounce this around." He tossed the soccer ball from one hand to the other, its alternating black and white patches spinning to a grey.

"Can a girl join?" asked Miriah.

"You gotta be kidding," said Brandon. "Just because we have a co-ed team doesn't mean—"

"Yeah, yeah, yeah," said Miriah. "I was kidding, just to see that look on your face. I've got other things to do. But I'll see you both at soccer practice after school."

"No, you won't," said Michael.

"Huh? You're not coming to practice?"

"No, Miriah. There is no practice. Today's the day we play O'Toole Elementary," said Michael. "Remember? Last night Ms. Wright announced that the schedule had been changed. Or were you too wrapped up in your orphans?"

"O'Toole? Omigosh, I forgot. They've got a good team. A friend of my says they've got a right winger—"

"Right wing is from hockey," said Brandon.

"Well, whatever. They won their first game 6–0. They've got a really good coach."

Brandon smiled. "Never fear, children dear. Their coach won't be on the field playing. And good old Parisotto Elementary has Michael the Striker to save the day."

"We're *that* good?" asked Miriah sarcastically.

"We're that good," said Brandon seriously.

3

Coaches' Battle

Where's Erika?" asked Ms. Wright.
          She stood on the touch line of Parisotto Elementary's soccer pitch. The playing area had been marked in white, with huge full-sized soccer goals at each end.

"She was at school today," said Victoria, snapping bubble-gum. "I saw her at noon."

Already, opponents from O'Toole Elementary huddled around the goal at the east end of the field. The few parents able to attend an after-school game were lined up along the west side of the field near the park.

Ms. Wright clasped her clipboard tighter. Her forehead took on little worry lines.

"She's the only goalie we have," she said.

"You don't think she's forgotten, do you? I almost did," said Miriah. "I can go look for her if you want."

Ms. Wright shook her head. The flecks of grey in her short-cropped hair reflected the sunlight. "We don't have time. The O'Toole team is here and ready to go. Erika was at school today? Whose class is she in?"

"She's in Mr. Tulley's class. Hey!" she yelled, "anybody seen Erika?" Several heads shook and several pairs of shoulders were shrugged.

"It doesn't matter anyhow," said Brandon. "We just give the ball to Michael and nobody else can touch it. We don't have to worry about a goalie."

Ms. Wright looked at Brandon. A slow smile grew. "You're right, Brandon," she said. "Why didn't I think of that? Thank you for solving our problem."

She rubbed out a name on her team list and replaced it with another, neatly printed in block letters. "Brandon, you're starting in goal."

"Me? Why me? Hey, I can't play goal. I'm a forward. Right forward. I play on the line with Michael, remember?"

Ms. Wright smiled. "But you said it doesn't matter. If we can put anybody in goal, then you can be anybody. We'll have to play one person short."

"That's okay, Brandon," said Michael. "This field is so short you should be able to score easy from goalie kicks."

From the centre of the field the referee — a teacher from another school dressed in a black-and-white zebra top and jeans — blew the whistle sharply and signalled the players into position.

"Okay, positions everyone," said Ms. Wright. "A little hustle. Brandon, I was serious about your being in goal. Let's get moving."

"You're serious?"

"Quite. Quit your moaning and let's go."

Brandon gave the coach one more pained look before he jogged over to the goal.

The referee tooted twice more on her whistle. Ms. Wright joined Michael at centre field with the opposing coach and centre forward for the coin toss.

"O'Toole wins," the referee said. She turned mildly red in the face as she gave another long blast on the whistle.

"Is this field regulation size?" Michael heard the opposing coach ask. "This field is not regulation size."

"The field is not regulation size," said Ms. Wright. "It's eighty metres long and forty metres wide. It also slopes down-hill from south to north. You knew that before you brought your team here, Ralph." The coaches walked to the edge of the field. Michael could hear no more of their conversation.

The centre mark, however, was regulation size. Michael backed up to the edge of the circle, about ten metres back. Because of the reduced size of the field, it brought him almost to the top of the penalty area.

The referee signalled to both sides. A nod to both captains, followed by a blast from her whistle, and game two of the regular season was on.

Michael braced for the kickoff shot that never came. The opposing captain had glared at him as though he would drill the ball through him and straight at Brandon in the goal. But instead of a direct kick, he lifted the ball high into the corner of the field; a kick aimed to drop before running out of bounds in the short field.

Michael retreated to help the backfielders keep possession. Pearly Hofstetter, one of the fifth graders on the team, got to the ball first. She kicked it down the line in a perfect clearing play.

But the pass was too perfect. The left forward on the O'Toole team had raced down the line expecting such a play. She intercepted, dribbled, and kicked the ball into the corner. She swivelled and chopped a short, high centring pass that came down almost at Brandon's feet.

Brandon rushed forward from the goal line to intercept. He missed. O'Toole's forward rushed in, caught the ball on his chest on the first bounce and raced around the baffled Brandon. He kept the ball close to his feet and literally ran through the goal.

The score: 1–0 for O'Toole.

"They planned that," said Brandon when he had regained the ball.

"No kidding," said Miriah. "What was your first hint?"

"Is that against the rules?" asked Kyle. "Is it?"

"What? The other team scoring a goal? You wish."

"They knew that it might work on this short field," said Michael. "We can't let them beat us on our own pitch."

"I don't call this a pitch," said Brandon. "It's more like a beginners lot. We played on fields this size when we were Tykes. Jeesh!"

The ball was centred again for the after-goal kickoff. Michael waited for the referee's whistle, checked that his forwards were onside, and rushed forward with a low kick. It was hard enough to score from center if it had gone that far.

Instead, the O'Toole forwards and midfielders expected it, and formed a compact wall to block the kick.

The ball caught one midfielder directly in the midsection. She made a funny sound, something like a balloon when you let go: the whooshing sound of escaping air along with the flapping of wind-blown lips.

"Oww! That hurt!" said Alysha from left midfield.

But the O'Toole team didn't hesitate. The ball bounced back behind Michael and the forwards to the midfield. The O'Toole forwards swarmed through like blackflies at a barbecue. The centre peeled the ball off Kyle's feet, swept by the two young backfielders, and kicked hard and low.

Brandon saw the play coming and moved out to cut the angle. The kick came in low to his outside. He made a superb dive to his left and caught the ball with the tips of his fingers before he thudded to the ground.

He groaned when he landed, his wind knocked free, and for a moment his fingers lost their grip. Recovering, he reached back in desperation, only to knock the ball further away with the back of his hand. The team watched in horror as the ball rolled slowly, gently nudging the right goal post, and came to rest just over the goal line.

O'Toole now led 2–0.

"We've got to focus," Michael said, as the referee placed the ball at centre for the kickoff.

"They prepared for our field," said Miriah.

"Short field, short game," said Brandon, coming up behind Michael. "They're ahead now. They're going to try to block so we can't score."

"That's what I would do," said Michael. "They're playing like this is indoor soccer."

"Indoor?" said Brandon. "You mean, like in a hockey rink?"

"Something like that, though we don't have the boards to bounce off. But shorter passes, quicker kicks."

"What can we do about that?"

"Not sure. Let's see."

Michael poised on his toes at the edge of the centre circle and waited for the referee's signal. He held his arms outstretched, like a diver ready to leave the high board. He checked his forwards on the left and right, and moved forward.

This time he struck the ball squarely and slightly below centre. It was a strong kick, high enough to just clear the wall of midfielders that the O'Toole team had created, hard enough that each member of that wall ducked as the ball flew over their heads.

The ball continued to rise on the short field until it cleared the goal at the far end and began to drop, bouncing fiercely once before it smashed through the branches of a maple tree and over the wire mesh fence into the yard next door.

"Time out!" signalled the referee, giving a toot on the whistle. "Do we have another ball?"

Another soccer ball was rolled onto the field. The referee signalled a goalie kick.

The field ran slightly uphill toward the Parisotto goal. The goalie booted the ball hard, just over the heads of the forwards and midfielders. It bounced twice and rolled to Brandon in goal.

"This could be a game of goalie kicks," said Michael.

Brandon scooped up the ball, ran forward with it three paces, and let go a drop kick; a high punt that soared overhead. Necks craned to watch its progress.

"Let's go!" yelled Michael. Instantly he saw Brandon's strategy. The high lob of the ball would allow the forwards time to race downfield and still be onside.

Michael and his two forwards sprinted ahead. The ball came down two metres in front of the O'Toole goal and bounced high. Michael headed the ball in mid-flight, bouncing it off the goal post.

"Rebound! Get the rebound!"

But a defending O'Toole backfielder cleared the ball from in front of the goal to the corner. A midfielder deked around Justin with the loose ball and headed up the field close to the touch line.

"Stop him!" yelled someone from the sidelines, as though it was an original idea.

In horror, Michael watched as both midfielders and back-fielders left their positions to converge on the ball carrier. Confronted with a wall of defenders, the O'Toole ball carrier turned and passed the ball back toward his own goal. A back-fielder took the pass on his left foot and immediately chipped a pass up the field on the opposite side, catching all the Parisotto defenders out of position. A dancing forward took the pass and raced toward the goal, where Brandon stood alone.

From centre field Michael could see the panicked look on

Brandon's face as the ball carrier bore down on him.

To give up a goal now would put them in a hole that would be difficult to dig out of. A three-goal deficit would leave the team deflated. He sprinted forward, determined to be on the heels of the attacker. *Let him make one mistake*, Michael thought, *and the ball is mine.*

The attacker continued toward the goal. Michael ran, one step behind, forcing him to hurry. From five metres out he pulled back his left foot for a hard kick.

Brandon, moving forward to try an interception, read the attack well. He sprinted forward and slid sideways on the hard-packed dirt. The ball caught him squarely in the face, and bounced back to Michael.

Michael picked up the ball and took off for the O'Toole goal. He dribbled around one midfielder, dipsy-doodled past a second. He circled and turned, keeping the ball close to his feet. This was his game now — in possession of the ball and closing on the goal.

Two backfielders, a guy and a girl, appeared between him and the goal. He headed toward them, then tromped down on the ball for side spin. The guy on the left moved to block him, but Michael had already changed direction. The girl held her position and tried to sweep forward with both feet to take the ball.

Michael pivoted easily around her and stared at the goalie, who stood transfixed. Behind him, he could hear the pounding of defenders.

From three metres out he booted a crisp, hard shot. The goalkeeper had no chance, didn't even try to move. Instead, she turned, and both she and Michael watched as the ball bounced once off the far goalpost and back out into the field.

* * *

At halftime Ms. Wright brought the team into a huddle.

"What's wrong?" she asked. "These guys are outplaying you."

"No kidding," said Brandon, his face still red from the smack he had taken.

"It's the short field," said Michael. "Their coach got them ready for this game by practising indoor tactics."

"What do you mean?" asked Ms. Wright. "I've never coached indoor soccer."

"Indoors you have to use short passes, run faster. You don't have space for fancy dribbling."

"You mean they keep the ball away from Michael," said Miriah, "so he doesn't take control."

"And notice how they swarm all over me, and form a wall in front of the goal," said Michael. "Even when I get the ball, I've got nowhere to go. On a full-sized field I'd have room to go around them."

"What can we do about it?"

Ms. Wright hushed the chatter around her. "Here's what we need to do. If they're going to swarm Michael, then we just have to get the ball to other people. Michael, when they swarm, they're all in front of you. There is only one direction you can safely pass."

"Back?"

"Yes. To midfielders, to Miriah and Victoria. Who can pass on to the opposite wing, where we have someone free. With the defenders all on the other side of the goal …"

"Okay. It'd work better if Brandon was playing forward."

A high-pitched voice interrupted as a girl ran full-tilt from the school, pulling the scarf from her hair as she sped toward them.

"I'm here!" said Erika. "Jeesh, I'm sorry I'm late. I didn't even know there was a game until I saw you guys out here."

"We had to change the game to fit it into the schedule," said Ms. Wright. "Erika, get in goal. I'll signal the referee about the changes. Brandon, you play left forward. Let's get it out there and get those two goals back!"

A blast from the referee's whistle summoned the teams back on the field.

4

A New Boy in Class

Michael was the school hero the next day.

"You were stupendous!" said Kyle, his red head bobbing. He was working on the bulletin board at the rear of the classroom, fitting class art into a display.

"What about me?" said Brandon. "If it wasn't for me and that diving save, they would have got up on us three to zip. Maybe *that* saved the game."

Miriah walked in the door, her arms filled with books. She slipped off her single-strap backpack. "It was obviously your modesty that saved the game, Brandon," she said, and everyone laughed.

"But 7–3." said Erika, adjusting her scarf. "I mean, Michael was awesome! Four goals! And he set up all the others. And I'm sorry I was late. I just didn't hear the announcement the night before."

"Well, it's a good thing you got there at halftime," said Miriah. "If Brandon stayed in goal all game it might have been 7–0 for O'Toole."

"You look like a farmer with that hankie in your hair," Brandon said to Erika.

"Brandon, you wouldn't know cool if it froze your butt," Erika replied.

Mr. Rahilly came into the classroom and pulled the door shut behind him. He was a tall man with ruffled hair and a frayed jacket that fit too small for him to button it properly. "Okay, people, time to settle down. It's almost time for the first bell. Into your seats. You, too, Kyle. You can finish that later." He spoke in an Irish accent that lilted like a sing-song washed up on ocean waves.

"I can't get them all in," Kyle said.

"Beg pardon?" said the teacher, as he slid a page into his lesson book and snapped the binder rings closed.

"All the art work from last class. I can't fit it all on the board. Can I use some of the side board?"

"It'll do you no harm to make adjustments," said Mr. Rahilly.

"But I'll have to cover up somebody's work," replied Kyle.

"You'll have to find a solution, Kyle. But do it later. Right now, take your seat."

The final bell rang, echoing up and down the halls. The Grade Seven class groaned to their feet while a scratchy version of the national anthem came over the tiny, tinny speaker. At the last chord, they creaked into their seats while two students from another class read the announcements over the PA system.

"Hope they remember to fit in an item about our soccer game," Brandon whispered, mainly to Kyle but loud enough for everyone to hear.

"Yeah, about your two goals," replied Kyle, also in a whisper. "It was nice of Michael to set you up like that."

Miriah turned and signalled to Michael, who sat two rows over and four seats back. "Tickets?" She mouthed the words, holding up a book of tickets and waving it back and forth.

"Working on it," Michael replied, his whisper barely loud enough to be heard.

"That's enough, people," said Mr. Rahilly. "Cut the chatter."

"What's the matter, can't fit ticket sales in your busy schedule?" whispered Erika, who sat closer to Michael. Her whisper was barely audible. The teacher frowned but said nothing.

When the announcements were over, the PA speaker gave several clicks, and some static, then gave way to an adult voice.

"Mr. Rahilly, it's Principal Moores here. I have a new student for your class. I'll be down to introduce him presently."

"Very good, Mrs. Moores," replied Mr. Rahilly, half hunched over the speaker while he flipped the talk-back button. He thought for a moment and scanned the room with his eyes. "It seems we will need another desk," he said. "Now if you two fine gentlemen would be so kind," he said, jabbing a finger at Brandon and Kyle each in turn. "Go seek out the custodian, Mrs. Yavanovich—"

"You mean Annie," said Kyle.

"Mrs. Yavanovich," repeated the teacher, stressing the name, "and tell her you need one more desk for our classroom."

"Is there room?" asked Brandon. "Can we fit it in?"

"That's no problem. Now to it, lads. Be quick. If you fall, don't wait to get up." He clapped his hands and the two were out the door.

In the next few minutes, Mr. Rahilly ordered the desks shifted to make one extra space in the row closest to the door.

"Please, sir, couldn't we put the new desk over by the windows?" asked Erika. "That'd give that group the same number as everybody else and let us stay together."

"You're putting on suspenders for ankle socks," replied the teacher. "We'll straighten that all out later. Right now I just want to have a desk for our new student."

There came a rap on the door. Without a wait for an answer, the door opened slowly. A tall woman dressed in a blue blazer, with glasses hanging from her neck, stepped in. Following her, a small, thin boy with dark hair and black eyes shuffled in, looking as though he would rather be invisible.

"Welcome, Mrs. Moores," said Mr. Rahilly. "And this must be our new student."

Before the principal could reply, Kyle and Brandon struggled up to the door. "Excuse us, please," said Kyle, walking backward, carrying the back end of a desk through the doorway.

"Watch your feet, watch your feet," said Brandon, lifting the front of the desk with his fingertips. "That's it."

"Right there in that corner," said Mr. Rahilly, pointing to the empty space that had been created. "There, that's fine. You've done a fine job and smartly, too. Now take your places."

While Brandon and Kyle returned to their seats, all eyes in the class shifted to where the newcomer stood behind the principal. His clothes were neat and clean but looked worn and too large on him. His jacket bore a Toronto Blue Jays crest.

"Class," said Mrs. Moores, when the class had settled, "I want to introduce you to Zahir Jamiat. Zahir, these are your new classmates."

The new boy peeked his head out from behind the principal. At the same time Mrs. Moores reached back as though to propel him forward, like a parent helping a student into the first day in Kindergarten.

The principal took a small step sideways and placed herself behind Zahir. As she opened the door, she said, "Zahir, Mr. Rahilly and his class will make you welcome. I'm sure you will find friends here." She backed out the door, closing it quietly.

The room was silent for a small crack in time. Surrounded by their eyes, the newcomer stood fixed in one spot, a frightened Bambi in a hunting party.

It was Brandon who broke the silence. "He's got Michael's

old jacket on." He meant to whisper, but his voice carried throughout the room. Brandon turned to Michael. "Isn't that the jacket you gave to—"

He did not have a chance to finish the sentence. Mr. Rahilly moved in to cut him off. But even the teacher was surprised when Zahir looked at the sleeve of his jacket — with the *old* logo on the chest — and someone giggled.

"We don't—" started the teacher.

The giggle tickled the tension in the room, and caused another. And another. The class broke down into giggles and laughter, and someone guffawed.

Michael watched as the new boy slid into the empty seat by the door. He looked as though he wished the earth would swallow him whole.

Thud.

Mr. Rahilly halted the laughter by bringing a large dictionary down forcefully on his desk.

"Ladies and gentlemen," he said, his voice subdued with anger. "This is not the way we greet newcomers to this class. To *my* class."

The laughter stopped abruptly. All eyes turned to the teacher. Silence squirmed.

"Zahir — have I pronounced it correctly? — let me apologize for this class of foolish buffoons."

The new boy dropped his eyes and nodded ever so slightly.

"Personally, I am ashamed," the teacher continued. "Many of you know the difficulty of joining a new class in a new school. And I can assure you, from my own personal experience of immigrating from Ireland when I was about your age, that moving to a new country with strange new customs is many times worse."

"Here he goes again," Brandon whispered to Michael. "The life story. He goes on and on and on."

"What does he mean by strange customs?" whispered Kyle.

"Mr. Sales and Mr. McIntyre," the teacher's voice broke in. "If you have anything to add, you can explain it to me in a private session after school."

"Sorry, sir," said Brandon.

"Sorry's not enough this time. Three-thirty today. Be here. Both of you."

In face of the teacher's anger, everyone's eyes dropped to study their own hands folded on their desks.

"Newcomers add richness," the teacher continued in his lilting voice. "This school is named after a man who moved to this country from Italy forty years ago. When I arrived in Canada, I had to give up my beloved football — that's the game you call soccer — for a country filled with ice hockey and softball. Two games, one barbaric and one silly."

He paused. Victoria, who was new to the school that year, raised her hand.

"You, sir? You played soccer?"

"I scored the winning goal in the under-twelve Ulster Minor Soccer Championship, in 1964," said Mr. Rahilly quietly. His face tightened and his jaw worked back and forth. "Then I never played again."

"Why, sir?" Michael asked.

"Because, Mr. Strike, when I came here, soccer teams were as rare as hen's teeth and as popular as Hallowe'en candy in a dentist's office."

"But," blurted Brandon, "more people play soccer than play hockey."

"That is true now," said Mr. Rahilly. "But back then, the only soccer teams were from the ethnic clubs: the Germans, the Italians, the Croatians. Ethnic clubs were set up after World War II, as many immigrants from those countries came here for a new life. In their clubs they were able to keep some of their customs. For many, that included soccer. The soccer you play today — yes, even the city rep team you play on, Mr. Strike — grew from that."

"Why wasn't there an Irish club?" asked Kyle.

"I was too late," replied the teacher. "Most Irish immigrants came to Canada 150 years ago, and they put their energy into playing games on ice — in the winter, when they had more time. Which brings us back to welcoming Zahir to our class. Zahir, forgive that digression. It is our way of saying that we understand the challenges you face. We'll do everything we can to help you adjust to this new class, in this new school, in this new country. Everyone here will help you."

Zahir gave a hesitant nod and a small smile. He said nothing.

Brandon waited until the teacher turned to the blackboard. "I told you he'd go on too long," he said under his breath, mainly to himself.

"Three-thirty, Mr. Sales," said the teacher without turning around.

5

Brandon's a Tease

One week later, Michael and Miriah were headed for soccer practice after school when Mrs. Moores stopped them.

"I have to see you both," she said. "Now."

"But we have soccer practice," Michael protested. "Can't it wait?"

"Ms. Wright will understand," said the principal. "We can meet in my office. Just go in. I'll be right there."

Michael and Miriah walked past the secretary's desk and took seats in the principal's office.

"I think you're really in for it now," Michael joshed.

"You, too," said Miriah. "How're your tickets sales going?"

"Uh, okay," Michael replied, avoiding her eyes.

The principal breezed in and sat down behind her desk. "This won't take a minute," she said. "It's about your fundraising."

"The War Orphans of the World?" said Miriah. "Is anything wrong?"

"No, no, it's a good idea," said the principal. "However, someone tried to sell tickets to a member of the school council."

"Is that a problem?"

"A minor one. The school council handles all of the school fundraising. So technically, your ticket sales have to be approved by the council."

"What's that mean?"

"Well, the next meeting of school council is Monday night. You'll have to make a presentation to them, tell them what you're doing, and why, and explain how you're handling the money collected. It's their way of making sure that all fundraising activities fit properly into the school. That they're for good causes, and don't interfere with one another."

"You mean not too many activities at a time?"

"Something like that. Once they've approved, it's pretty much business as usual."

"Pretty much?"

"They may want to provide some adult help in keeping track of the money," said the principal. "That's all."

"They don't trust us," Michael blurted.

"They'll likely want to help in some way. I don't know exactly how they'll react. But you do have to prepare a presentation. Do you think you two are up to that?"

"Us two?" said Michael. "This is Miriah's project. I'm just selling tickets."

"Or promising to," said Miriah. "I can make the presentation myself."

"It would be better if there were two of you," said the principal. "It would look stronger as a group activity than a one-person campaign."

"I'll be there," said Miriah, gathering up her sweater.

"Michael?" said Mrs. Moores.

Michael looked from one to the other. Miriah glared back at him in a combination of defiance and pleading.

"If …" Michael hesitated. "If it will help … Miriah has to do all the talking."

"Monday night, seven-thirty. See you there," said the principal.

In the foyer they found Zahir standing near the far wall,

examining the mural of photographs the Grade Two class had made.

"Hi, Zahir," said Miriah.

"Chess club?" Zahir asked, pointing to the stage.

"That's where they meet," Michael said, speaking slowly, the way he would to a small child. "They meet there at noon."

After a full day in class, this was the first time they heard Zahir speak. Mr. Rahilly has spent time with him in class, one-on-one, but Zahir had yet to take part in class discussion.

"Then I will come back at noon." Zahir had an English accent, mixed with something else Michael could not place.

"At noon," Michael repeated.

"Yes. Thank you." Zahir turned and walked away. He shuffled, as though unsure of the direction he was going. Michael thought he began to turn back to them once, as though he would ask another question.

Outside in the sunlight, Michael turned to Miriah. "That ought to make Cachuk happy. Someone interested in chess."

"But you play chess!"

"I quit. Not enough challenge."

"Is there anything else you can't do?"

"I'm not that good at chess. And there are too many young kids playing."

"You could help out, like Mr. Cachuk asked you to," she said. "We should all help where we can."

Michael shrugged. "You sound like my mom," he said. "Besides, I'm busy with soccer."

* * *

At soccer practice that afternoon, Ms. Wright had the players dribbling soccer balls in figure-eights around the field.

"Grab a ball and join the fun," Ms. Wright said. "Up and down the field."

Michael dribbled the ball for a few metres before Miriah appeared before him and tried to block him. He took control, pulling the ball in behind his heels.

"You going to play keep-away for the whole practice?" asked Miriah. "Or do we all just stand around and admire how good Michael is?"

Michael stopped for a moment and looked at Miriah. Her green eyes would not let him go.

"Have you ever heard the word 'share' before?" Miriah continued. "It's part of teamwork."

Michael shrugged. "Sorry," he said. "Here. What we can do is this. You take the ball up and down the field. I'll play defence, and you try to get around me."

"Yeah, sure, Mr. Kicks."

"No, I mean it. It'll give you practice at dribbling the ball. Try it."

Miriah took the ball and started toward Michael. Michael placed himself about two metres away, between her and the goal behind him.

"See, a good defender will keep that distance, try to make you commit yourself," he said. "On the other hand, what you want to do is keep control and either break away or find a clear teammate to pass to."

"Well, yeah," Miriah said, her face blank but her voice smiling.

"That's it. Keep the ball close to your feet. Unless you kick out to go around me. But then make sure you're still between the ball and the defender. It's better to turn around and go back than lose the ball."

"How's this?"

"Better. Good. Have you played much?"

Miriah shook her head. "I've never played on the school team before. Just in gym class. Last year this team lost every game."

"That's what Erika said."

"So I saw that picture of you in the paper. Until then I didn't know you played soccer."

"That's when you asked me to try out?"

Miriah smiled. "I knew the team needed somebody." She stopped and looked at Michael. "I was right. Just don't get stuck up and all."

Michael grinned. "Brandon was right."

"What do you mean?"

"He said you're always trying to save the world. Or, in this case, the soccer team. And the school."

Miriah laughed. "Well, I wouldn't quite put it like that. But somebody has to try to make things happen."

"That's what my coach says. He says if you're in the game you may as well kick the ball."

"The coach of the Kicks? Are you playing with them again?"

"Yeah, we had tryouts weeks ago. Hey, that's good. Try that move again."

"This okay?"

"Good!" he said. "As soon as I get too close, that's when you have the chance. If I commit myself to tackle you, that gives you a chance. Chip it out and go around. That's it!"

After a few minutes of drill, Ms. Wright gave another long blast on her whistle. When the team had gathered around her, she signalled for attention.

"We've played four games," she said. "Who would have believed it? You guys are undefeated."

"Playoffs, here we come!" said Erika.

Ms. Wright smiled and continued. "We play next Tuesday against either Coronation or Donevan at the Civic Fields. The winner of that game will play for the city championship at the new fields at the University of Ontario and Durham College."

"We're ready," said Brandon. "Meet the new city champs!"

"Don't count your chickens before you know where the nest is," said Ms. Wright.

"Yeah, but we got Michael on our side," said Brandon. "Nobody else has talent like that."

"And why do you say that, Brandon?" Ms. Wright asked. "The further we go, the more likely we are to run into a team with one or two players from Michael's team. How many teammates did you have on the Kicks team last year, Michael?"

Michael, caught unaware by the questions, mumbled, "Huh? Oh, I dunno. Seventeen. Yeah, we were eighteen altogether."

"And these players are all your age and live in Oshawa?"

"Well, they don't all live in Oshawa, but yeah, they're all about my age."

"So there you go, Brandon. Maybe there are a dozen other players out there who could show up on one of the teams we play. What happens if we end up with a team that has two Michaels on it? Or three? What then?"

Brandon shrugged.

"You are a team," said Ms. Wright. "No matter how good one individual is, teamwork is more important. You can't all rely on Michael to do all the work. You saw that game with O'Toole. If a team decides to swarm Michael, then Michael's job is to get the ball to the rest of the team. So let's work on that."

Brandon kicked at a loose bottle cap. "But why would those guys want to play on a school team? I mean, if they've been on a Kicks championship team why would they bother?"

"Ask Michael," said Ms. Wright. "Why does he bother to play for a school team?"

"To show off for the girls," Brandon said, and everybody laughed.

"What do you mean?" said Ms. Wright before she joined the laughter.

"Maybe you should ask Miriah," said Brandon. "He's got the hots for Miriah."

Michael turned a strange colour of red. Miriah turned away.

"Okay, team," said Ms. Wright. "Positions. We're going to do a little corner-kick drill."

6

More Teasing

The corner kick is an advantage given to an attacking team," Ms. Wright said. "It is granted when the defending team is the last to touch the ball before it goes over the goal line without scoring."

She placed a soccer ball in the corner of the pitch even with the goal line.

"You mean like if the goalie stops a shot and keeps it out," stated Brandon.

"Something like that. The attacking team gets to kick from the corner. You can score on a corner kick but, as you can see, you'd have to kick a wonderful curve."

"Bend it," said Alysha.

"Yeah, ever see the pros," said Brandon. "The way they can curve that corner kick so it comes right in on goal?"

"Michael, I bet you can do that," said Kyle.

"Back to our drill," said Ms. Wright. "It's better to pass to a teammate who is in position to score. Now where might that teammate be?"

"In front of the goal," said Miriah, surprising everyone.

"Right. So when your team is given a corner kick, where should the forwards be?"

Hands waved as though they were in a classroom. "Please,

Ms. Wright," said Justin, "in front of the goal."

"And the midfielders?"

"Up to the penalty area?" said Kyle. "Ready to score?"

"That would do. And your backfielders?"

"Hanging back at midfield," said Kyle.

"Why's that?"

"Just in case."

"In case why?"

"In case the other team gets the ball!"

"Okay. Let's try it."

Even on their small, narrow field, most players couldn't make the kick to the front of the goal. Brandon tried and did better than most, his kick soaring high but coming down amid the defenders.

"On full-sized fields that's going to be even more of a problem," said Ms. Wright. "Just remember, you don't have to play the long ball from the corner. You can play a short ball by passing to a teammate." She rolled the ball toward the corner. "Michael, do you want to show us how to do it?"

Michael lined up the ball in the corner. He waited until the attackers and defenders got in position. He booted the ball high and watched as it curved slightly toward the goal. Brandon had positioned himself well in front. He burst forward as the ball came down, catching it on first bounce, heading the ball into the goal.

"That's picture perfect," said Ms. Wright. "Now let's practise some more. And Kyle, could you work a bit more with Justin?"

"Do I have to? The little kids are a pain."

Ms. Wright answered him with a look.

After practice, Miriah helped Michael round up the soccer balls to take back into the school.

"Monday night's that presentation to school council," she said. "We've got to get to work on that."

"*You've* got to get to work on it," Michael replied. "I'm just there for company, remember?"

"Oh, yeah, I forgot. It's the caveman thing: you're big and strong and too stupid to say anything."

"I said I'd be there."

"And I will do the presentation," said Miriah. "But we do need to work on it together. Somebody might ask you a question."

"Question?" Michael had not thought of that possibility.

"If I get it done on the weekend, will you help me go over it Monday at noon? We could meet at the stage."

"During lunch? Sure." Michael hesitated, scuffed his shoes on the floor. "Sorry about that dumb thing Brandon said."

Miriah looked at him. "I'm not," she said. As she turned to leave, she gave him her big-toothed smile.

As the team struggled to put the bouncing soccer balls into the storage nets in the equipment room, Ms. Wright gave one last reminder: "Remember, Tuesday's the next game. If we win, we make it to the finals."

* * *

As he promised, Michael met Miriah at noon the following Monday to review the presentation.

"It's too noisy up here," said Miriah. She jerked her thumb to the main section of the stage, where the chess club appeared locked in a royal battle. One younger student was throwing chess pieces about. Another was doing a convincing imitation of a chimpanzee, complete with underarm scratching movements.

"Mr. Cachuk isn't here," said Michael. He drew the privacy curtain, separating off part of the stage. It did nothing to muffle the sound of the chaos, but now they could not see it.

"That does heaps," said Miriah.

"Let's just get this thing done. Did you get it all down last night?"

"I put it all on a computer presentation. Then I thought that might look too slick."

"Besides, we'd have to set it all up before the meeting."

"That's what I thought. I have the notes all printed out ..." A chess piece skidded along the floor under the curtain and came to rest by Miriah's foot. "... so I thought we'd just go with that."

"We'd?" queried Michael.

"We. You can hold up the cards. Smile. That sort of thing. Look pretty." She gave him a friendly forced smile. Michael didn't know whether he was being insulted or flirted with.

Miriah spread the printed displays out on the small desk.

"You certainly have prepared," said Michael. "You've done a lot of work."

"It would be—"

The curtain fluttered and a head poked up from beneath. "You guys seen a chess piece come flying?" asked Justin, just his head and two arms visible under the curtain.

"Here," said Michael, tossing him the stray King. "You kids sure are loud this year."

"Yeah, thanks. Hey, you gonna come out and play some, Mike?"

Michael shook his head. "Name's Michael," he said, "And the answer's no."

The younger boy wiped his wrist across his chin. "How about some simul?" In his first couple of months of attending the chess club, Michael had taken to playing simultaneous chess against younger members of the team.

"Another time. I'm busy."

Justin's head disappeared, his arm the last part of him to go, sliding under the bottom of the curtain still clutching the stray black King. Almost immediately, the head reappeared under the curtain.

"Michael?"

"Yeah?"

"That new guy."

"What new guy?"

"The new guy in your class. The one from another country."

"Zahir?"

"Yeah, that's it. He any good?"

"What do you mean? Any good at what?"

"At chess. He's here to play today. Think he's any good?"

"I have no idea. Play him and find out. Now let us get some work done."

Miriah smiled patiently. "And I thought chess was a quiet sport." Michael shrugged.

"So let's go over this presentation," Miriah said. "One more time."

Fifteen minutes later, after Miriah had completed the talk twice, they pulled the curtain back, intending to head outside. Michael wanted to join his friends on the playground. Standing in the middle of the lobby was Brandon.

"Hey, hey!" he said. "What have you two been up to behind the curtain?"

Michael and Miriah tried to ignore the taunt, but Brandon wouldn't let up. He walked with Michael out to the playground, all the while chanting a little ditty he thought was cute:

Michael and Miriah, sitting in a tree,
K-I-S-S-I-N-G

First comes love, then comes marriage,
Then comes Miriah with a—

"All right, all right, shut up," Michael said at last. "What, are you in the second grade, you dumb dork."

7

Michael's Injury

In the sunken soccer field behind the Civic Stadium, Tarcisio Parisotto Elementary School met Coronation Elementary in the city school soccer championship semi-finals.

"Look at this, Michael," said Brandon, as they jogged out onto the field. "You'll have lots of room to run here."

Michael shrugged. He had played on this field many times. In fact, the Kicks had often practised here. The grandstand, which faced the 400-metre track and football field, appeared to have turned its back on them. He also knew that the pitch, lower than the upper field and parking lot, collected water. It had rained the night before, and the eastern corners would be sloppy. Perhaps the whole field would be muddy.

The game had attracted a small group of spectators: some parents, a few students from each school, and a photographer from the community newspaper.

"Eww, this is uck, wet," said Erika, as she crossed the corner of the field, tying her blue bandana in place. "I hope it's not like this in front of the goal."

The mud and water had dampened the pre-game warm up. The promise of mid-May warm sunshine had disappeared. Low dark clouds scudded across the sky. Many players on the touch line were shivering in the brisk breeze.

Ms. Wright gathered the team around her. "We've won some good games this year," she said. "Let's get out there and give this our best shot."

"Championship, here we come!" said Brandon.

"Yeah, yeah," said several of his teammates, not quite as enthusiastically.

"Don't look too far ahead," said Ms. Wright. "Let's just concentrate on this game, okay?"

"Go get 'em Michael!" Brandon said, filling a small silence.

"And remember, Michael, that you have teammates. You don't have to do everything yourself."

"Okay."

The referee's whistle blew, one long blast with a dip in the middle that told them the game was to begin.

Erika won the coin toss against the Coronation captain. This gave Coronation the first kick off, but meant that Parisotto would kick off to begin the second half.

The opening kick was lofted over the heads of the forwards. Victoria, playing midfield, stopped the ball at the top of the penalty area and kicked it along the ground to Michael.

Michael dipped around the opposing centre and picked up the ball. He dodged and swerved, the ball at his feet, as two Coronation players converged on him. He smiled at them and ragged the ball between his feet, challenging them.

They took the bait. Both players lunged toward him, one on each side. With the edge of his foot he tipped the ball to his right, while he faked a body move to the left. When both opponents reacted to the fake, he jerked back clear of both defenders, kicking the ball ahead with easy control.

He caught the midfielders standing and was around them in less time than it would take to do up their shoe laces.

He continued upfield. A long boot while dribbling fooled

the backfielders. Three defenders rushed forward to get what they saw was a free ball. But Michael was there before them, almost smirking as he watched them try now to reverse directions. Too late. He was past them.

The Coronation goalkeeper took three steps forward and planted his feet, far enough out to cut the angles, not so far out that Michael could easily go around him. He played the position well, Michael thought, wondering if he could react as well.

He checked for teammates. Behind him he could hear defenders trying to run him down. He moved sideways to his right, watching as the goalkeeper ran with him to keep the angles covered. A good move, but not quite fast enough.

Michael brought back his right foot and kicked, hard.

The ball plunked off his foot. Michael watched it soar. The goalie dove, but missed, and the ball bounced off the right post into the goal, ruffling the draped netting.

"Attaboy, Michael!" said Brandon, offering a high-five.

"Way to go!" said Kyle.

"Nice goal," said Miriah, offering a gentler knuckle wrap.

Michael knew it would be a good game.

* * *

Tarcisio Parisotto Elementary School went into the second half of the game nursing a lead of 5–3. Michael had scored four goals. He could have scored the fifth, but as he closed in on an open net he had spotted Brandon to his left. Michael had fed him a pass that Brandon almost mishandled before he tipped the ball across the line.

Michael took the kickoff for the second half, connecting well and watching the ball soar toward the Coronation goal. It bounced once over the heads of the backfielders. The goalie rushed forward, scooped up the ball, and took two long paces to the edge of the penalty area to drop the ball for a long punt.

At least, that's what the goalie intended to do. But instead of delivering the punt, he missed. His feet slipped out from under him.

Michael rushed forward to take advantage of the error. Before he could reach the ball, one backfielder rushed in and booted the ball toward the corner. Michael followed the kick. He watched as the ball splashed through the puddles in the corner of the field.

Michael beat his own left forward into the corner. Under his feet he could feel the splash of water, the squish of mud and dampness. He tried to pull to a stop to bring the ball under control. Instead, his left foot skidded forward in the mud. His right foot came up. The next thing he knew he was — *splat!* — facedown in a hidden puddle in the grass, his right foot under him awkwardly.

He was up again in an instant, on the ball and controlling it, dribbling around one, two backfielders. Spinning free, he lobbed a pass high into the penalty area where Miriah — playing midfield aggressively — waited.

As soon as he kicked the pass, he knew that his right foot was not right. The twinge ran up his leg. The ball bounced to Justin, who had doggedly planted himself in front of the opposition goal. The small boy kicked at the pass and missed, then turned to watch as Miriah scored, taking the pass on her instep and redirecting the ball into the empty half of the goal.

Michael exchanged high-fives with all his teammates within reach. He jogged back to the centre of the field, trying not to let his limp show.

"Are you all right?" Miriah asked.

"It's nothing," he said. "I just need to walk it off, that's all."

"I almost scored! I almost scored!" said Justin, jumping up and down.

Michael patted him on the head. "Keep in there," he said. "Doin' good." He walked and jogged until the pain disappeared. He could dribble and run and pass with no problem. It was not until he was awarded a free kick from near centre that he knew that something was still wrong.

He approached the ball at a hard run, three-quarters speed, and put full weight into the kick. The ball soared toward the Coronation goal, and his own forwards pounced on it. Instead of following them, Michael grasped his shin and winced. The pain was sharp, his leg, when he added weight, now weak.

"Are you all right?" asked Miriah again, this time more concerned. Little worry lines appeared on her forehead.

"A twinge," he said, hopping down the field with a skippity hop that resembled Terry Fox's hop-hop-skip gait. The running massaged the pain, easing it out his toes until soon he could hardly feel it.

Nevertheless, as the Parisotto team cruised to a 7–4 victory, Michael nursed his right foot, making all his kicks with his left foot and passing to teammates instead of dribbling in to score.

He was sure that no one noticed.

8

School Council

Tarcisio Parisotto felt different at night. Looking from the foyer down dimly lit hallways, Michael could see shadows. Far down the hall, near the library, he saw the glint of the custodian's scrub cart.

The gymnasium lurked — eerily silent, dark and mysterious. This was not the same nighttime face the school showed during Parents Night, or Book Fair Week, or Meet-the-Teacher Night, when students, parents, and teachers bustled through the building. No, this was School Council Night, quiet as a graveyard, the only sound the ghostly rattling of the scrub cart.

"I thought that there'd be a big crowd here," said Miriah, flipping through her presentation pages.

"Dad says nobody shows up because nobody wants to be elected to do anything," said Michael. "He was going to be here but he had to work late." Michael's father sold investment certificates, mutual funds, and stock options. He was always busy making lots of money.

"My mom was going to be here," Miriah said. "But tonight's the annual meeting of the Oshawa Symphony Board."

"My mom dropped me off on her way to the gym," Michael said. "She always says she's going to do stuff. But she doesn't."

Mrs. Moores came out of the office. "We're meeting in the

staff room," she said. "There should be someone in there. Make yourself at home." She left.

Michael and Miriah wandered through the small kitchenette that doubled as an entry to the staff room. Someone had started a huge urn of coffee, which bubbled and burped and gave off coffee odours.

"Come on in, come on in," said a woman in a big, loud, outdoor voice. "No use dawdling if you can rush right in."

A small woman with very black hair, a dark complexion, and friendly eyes came forward, right arm outstretched for handshakes. She was dressed in jeans and a denim jacket. "I'm Mrs. Mitchell," she said, "but you may call me Martie. You must be our student delegation. You're the Strike boy, right? David and Lisa's son. I know them well. And you're Miriah. I don't think I know your parents. Anyway, we're so glad to see you. Now, you two just grab yourself a seat and help yourself to the cookies."

Three other women and two men were gathered around the long table. Three separate plates of home-made cookies were within easy reach of every seat.

"That's a seat each, you don't have to share one," said Mrs. Mitchell. "We have plenty of room." The other adults chuckled the way adults chuckle when dealing with very young children. "These other people will introduce themselves."

The others in the room half rose and gave Michael and Miriah half handshakes.

"Our kids are all in the early grades," said one woman. "I wonder what happens to parents when their kids get older."

"Kids don't want 'em involved," said one man. "Embarrasses them."

"Well, you're going to embarrass these two," said a woman, perhaps his wife.

"How about those Leafs," said the other man, a big hearty man wearing a baseball cap. "Think they'll make it?"

The Toronto Maple Leafs had started off the National Hockey League playoffs with great promise. But this spring, as every year, playoff injuries threatened their chances to finally win the Stanley Cup.

"Maybe," Michael said.

"Their biggest problem is goaltending," said Miriah. "They're one injury away from having nothing. And for years they've suffered from poor defence. But this year they'll make it to the next round at least."

"Ho," said the man in the cap, "an optimist."

"All Leafs fans are optimists, Doug," said one of the women.

Five more adults entered the room. "This where we come to keep the school open?" one asked.

"It's the school council meeting," said Mrs. Mitchell. "And that's one thing we are going to talk about. Pull up some chairs, you people. Doug, would you mind getting some from off the stage?"

Doug had been tilting his chair back on two legs. He rocked forward with a plunk, adjusted his baseball cap, and stood. "It'll just take a minute," he said.

"Your soccer team is doing very well this year," said Mrs. Mitchell, in the shuffling that followed. Michael wondered how such a big voice could belong to such a small woman. "The big game for the city championship is coming up next week."

"Wednesday," said Miriah, "at the university fields."

"Woo-wee! Championship, here we come!" said Mrs. Mitchell. "We'd all be at that game, but that's the day we have to make a presentation to the school board about the school closing. Anybody like anything to drink? We've got coffee, tea

— hey, maybe that's not right. Do we have soda pop? Maybe there's some orange juice we can serve up. Or would you rather have milk?"

"No thanks," Michael said, wondering where Mrs. Mitchell found the phrase "soda pop."

"Here's Doug with the chairs. So if everybody could just move around a bit. That's it. Yes, that'd really be great," said Mrs. Mitchell. "To win a championship. That way we'd show them the power of small schools! You two have heard about the board wanting to close this school? Of course you have. Everybody has. Well, one of the jobs of this school council is to convince them otherwise. This school has been around for years and years. We're not going to stand around and let them do it."

"I went to this school," said Doug as he returned to his chair and tilted back again. "Way back."

"It'd have to be way back, Doug," said the other man. They both laughed.

"We'll get our meeting started as soon as Mrs. Moores gets back. Oh, here she is. Okay, then, let's get started. Does everyone have an agenda?"

Mrs. Moores slid a sheet of paper to Michael and another to Miriah with the agenda.

"So first," continued Mrs. Mitchell. "Is everyone in favour of the agenda? No problems? That's great, then I'll take a motion to accept it. Notice that item at the end, New Business — if you have stuff you want to bring up then, you can do so, even if it's not on the agenda. When we do that I wonder why we have to approve the agenda in the first place.

"Okay, moving right along. Minutes of the last meeting. Did everybody get the minutes we sent around? Anybody noticed any errors or stuff like that? No? Great. Then somebody can move that we accept the minutes. Doug? Great. That was Mr.

Sthankiya. Did I say that right? And a seconder? Fine. Hey, we're making great time tonight."

She cleared her throat quickly.

"Now, usually, we go over these minutes with a fine-tooth comb for business arising from the minutes. But tonight we're going to put that off until later and jump right to number seven on the agenda, the student delegation. That way these fine young people can make their presentation and get on their way. Everybody okay with that? Right. So. Michael Strike and Miriah Bushra. Now, before you begin, perhaps there's something about us that you should know. This is the school council. We're named by other parents to represent all school parents.

"So. School policy is that school council handles all fundraising. That's so we don't have every class out trying to raise money, competing with each other, that sort of thing. We're told you're doing some fundraising, so we want to know how it might fit. Now's the time you tell us all about it. You're on."

All eyes swivelled to Michael. Embarrassed, he dropped his eyes.

Miriah stood up.

Mrs. Mitchell raised her hand one moment to interrupt. "I know these presentations can make you nervous," she said. "But just relax. We're all your friends here." She gestured with her open hand. "You're on."

"There are . . ."

"Just so we can keep this informal, do you mind if we ask questions as you go along?"

Miriah nodded. Again, she began: "There are more than 100 million orphans in the world today," she began. "Many are the victims of war, of famine, of disease — all things that we in the richest countries can help solve."

She paused and looked each person in the eye before continuing.

"But it is the war orphans that I am most concerned with, in countries like Iraq, Afghanistan, and Bosnia, where most of the help available to orphans has also been destroyed. That is why fundraising such as we are proposing is so important. . ."

Michael listened while Miriah continued. Even before she was a minute into the presentation, he was sure that she would win approval from the school council.

9

A Second Chance

The following morning Michael arrived in class before Miriah. The first bell had not yet sounded. Mr. Rahilly sat at his desk at the front of the room straightening piles of papers, getting ready for the day of classes.

"A top of the marnin' to ya," he said, as Michael slouched to his desk and shuffled off his backpack.

"Morning," Michael replied. Most of the time Mr. Rahilly's Irish accent was barely detectable. At other times he seemed to thicken it so his voice resembled a tourist commercial.

"And how would ya be keeping this marnin'?" asked the teacher. "And how did your presentation go last night?"

Michael looked up. The first bell sounded. Other students entered the classroom.

"Miriah got stonewalled," he said. "They listened all polite and everything. Then when she got to the end, they asked her to put it all in writing. What a waste of time! Why couldn't they have said no right off? It's chicken dirt."

"So you figure they won't go for it?" asked Erika as she slid into her desk across the aisle.

"It's dead as a dormouse," said Michael.

"You mean doornail," said Erika.

Zahir slipped almost unnoticed into his seat by the door.

"Whatever," said Michael. "They're not gonna go for it, that's for sure."

"What's the matter, Michael Strike? Somebody kick you in the head?" said Miriah as she flounced into the room. "The fund drive for War Orphans of the World is definitely on. How could you ever get the impression otherwise?" She smiled at Zahir, and waved to the others in the class.

"Hi, guys," she said. "Morning and all that, like, sunshine stuff."

Michael felt like a child being scolded.

"Well, I thought ..." He halted. "They asked you for a written report, for cripes sake. A written report. I mean, you were there, and they—"

The final bell sounded. Mr. Rahilly clapped his hands. The room fell silent, gradually, until the opening exercises crackled out of the tired intercom. After the announcements, Mr. Rahilly broke up the five different conversations that had begun.

"Before we get at it for the day," he said, "perhaps Miriah could tell us what happened last night. At the school council presentation."

"Nothin'," said Michael. "She got turfed."

"That doesn't seem to be how Miriah saw it," said the teacher. "So perhaps Miriah and Michael can explain and tell us why they disagree."

Miriah rose to her feet. "The council listened while I told them all about War Orphans of the World. I told them the same things almost that I told you guys. I told them that, after I finished the research, I knew somebody had to do something, so I started selling raffle tickets to raise money."

"Way to go!" said Erika.

"She did a great job," said Michael. "But it didn't get her

anywhere. They just flicked her off like a piece of lint and that was that."

Miriah turned to Michael. "They just asked if we would put it all in a written report. We have to get it done by Wednesday. As soon as we get it to them, we'll know the answer right away."

"Write a report. That sounds like a stonewall to me," said Michael.

"Hold it, hold it, hold it," said Mr. Rahilly. "We may have a teachable moment here. Ms. Bushra, do you have the material for your presentation in any readable form?"

Miriah nodded. "Well, yeah. I had them in a computer presentation. Then I scrapped that, figuring it would look too canned. But I printed out the pages of point-form notes. You don't think I was going to wing it, do you?"

"No," said Mr. Rahilly, "not you, Miriah, although many others might try that." He turned his gaze directly on Michael, who tried to shrug it off.

"They could have just said no," Michael said. "And saved us a lot of trouble. Why—"

"I take it, Mr. Strike, that you'd prefer to give up a goal than to take a corner kick."

"What do you mean? I didn't say anything about that."

"You seem to say a lot of things indirectly that you don't mean to say," said the teacher. "Now this report that you and Ms. Bushra are to do for the school council …"

"Miriah and me? Whoa, just a minute. I don't mind helping out here, like selling tickets if we're allowed. And it is a good idea. To help other people. But this report is just a waste of time. They've already decided to say no."

"Thanks a lot, Michael," Miriah said. "Here I thought you were a real team player."

"Hey, I was there," said Michael.

"Sure. The silent cheerleader," said Miriah.

"It's just that it's useless," Michael replied. "They're all tied up with fighting the school board over the closing."

"So useless that I'm asking Miriah to bring her notes this afternoon," said Mr. Rahilly. "We'll use today's English class to delve into the beauty and structure of the business report."

"Aww, sir!" said Brandon.

" 'Aww,' to you, too, Mr. Sales," replied the teacher. "Don't let Mr. Strike baffle you. Mr. Strike, can you explain to the class what a corner kick is?"

Michael sat up straight, taken by surprise.

Brandon interrupted. "Mr. Rahilly, how come with all you know about soccer, you're not coaching the team? Ms. Wright has never even played soccer."

"And she's doing a fine job," said Mr. Rahilly. "You will recall that this is my first year at this school."

"And maybe the last," said Kyle," "for all of us."

"There's that. But if it weren't for people like Ms. Wright stepping up when necessary, many good things would not happen. Now Michael here was going to define a corner kick for us."

"I don't get it."

"Don't get what, Mr. Strike?"

"What you're getting at. First we're talking about reports and war orphans, and now we're talking about soccer. Did I miss something?"

"Let's just say it's my Irish temperament, Mr. Strike. Humour me. If you kick on goal, and don't score, the goalie has knocked the ball out of bounds."

"Did I kick on goal?" he asked.

"Let's suppose you did. You and Miriah."

"The attackers get a corner kick."

"For those who don't follow soccer. Define it."

"Well," Michael halted for a moment. Explaining something that you understood very well, he had learned, can be the trickiest thing to do. "The attacker places the ball in the corner of the field, even with the goal line. One attacker gets to kick from that position."

"Attempting to do what?"

"Well, score if you can kick hard enough, and can curve the ball in toward the goal. But only the pros can do that. The best is to pass to a teammate who can score, or set up a scoring play. Yeah, that's it."

"Set up a scoring play. Very good. But you still don't see the parallel, do you Mr. Strike?"

"You lost me."

"Mr. Strike." The teacher's voice was calm and patient. And firm. "You and Ms. Bushra had a great opportunity last night. But for some reason, that did not happen. Maybe it would have helped if you had shown a little teamwork, that both of you had been involved in the presentation."

"But it was Miriah's idea," Michael protested.

"Which everyone in the class agreed to support," said Mr. Rahilly. "That makes it a team effort."

"But the school council said ..."

"Yes, the written report: don't think of that as failure. It is a corner kick. You've got possession again — and a great opportunity: to win the request to sell tickets to raise money for the War Orphans of the World."

The class was silent for a moment. It was hard to tell whether they were stunned quiet or happy quiet.

In the corner by the door, one hand rose slowly.

"Yes, Zahir?"

All eyes in the class turned.

"Sir," said Zahir, the first time he had spoken in class. His voice came out reed thin with a crisp British accent. "I would be very happy to learn more about this War Orphans project, and to help with it."

10

Zahir's Talents

At practice that afternoon — two days before the championship game — Justin ran out to the soccer practice field with startling news.

"It's Zahir!" he yelled. "Zahir beat Mr. Cachuk in chess today!"

"He what?" Kyle asked. "You mean, beat him in an even game?"

"Sure did. Just plunk, plunk, plunk. No more than twenty moves. Cachuk just sat there staring at the board when it was over, shaking his head."

"What? Speed chess?" asked Michael. "Or simultaneous?" Cachuk often played several players at the same time, moving from board to board. Michael had beaten him once in such a game, but it wasn't like a real game with someone's full concentration. He thought Cachuk couldn't have been trying too hard.

"No simul," said Justin. "They used a clock and everything, and took almost the whole noon hour. And Cachuk was really trying, that's for sure."

"Come on, come on, come on," said Ms. Wright, clapping her hands. "We've got a big game in two days. No time to stand around and chatter!"

The team was still doing warm-ups. Michael grabbed a ball and began dribbling up the field with it. First Kyle popped up in front of him, flapping his arms out sideways as though that would stop him. Michael kept the ball close to his feet, stopped, spun, and reversed direction, leaving Kyle with his jaw slack.

Justin and Alysha appeared next. Obviously, stopping Michael Strike had become the fad of the day. He quickened his pace, kicked long, and went around them, taking the ball into the corner.

Brandon pulled up beside him, veering toward the goal where Erika was taking practice shots.

"Here!" he called. "Pass it here."

Michael saw Brandon jumping up and down near the goal. But Michael was not in the mood for fancy passing plays or teamwork. He spun the ball at his feet and dribbled closer to the goal, coming out of the corner with fire in his eyes.

Erika turned to him now, prepared to block a practice kick.

Michael looked up, his jaw set. Now he could see the focus in Erika's eyes as she watched Michael approach. He moved in closer, around Brandon. He felt fuelled by anger, but didn't know where it came from.

From three metres out he touched the ball, rolling it a metre ahead. He bounded toward it, building speed, and pulled his right foot back for a blistering kick.

Erika saw his intention and moved toward him, bringing her left foot out in a wide sweep in an attempt to steal the ball.

Michael ignored her. He continued with his kick at full power, his right instep catching the ball squarely.

The pain shot through his lower leg like an electric shock. The power kick turned into a weak punt that a falling Erika caught in two arms as she went down. Michael flopped to the field, grabbed his right shin in both hands, and rolled.

"You okay, Michael?" asked Erika, who got to her feet first.

"I thought you'd put that one over the fence," Brandon said. "You looked like you were really about to boot it."

"Are you okay?" Erika repeated. Michael got to his feet, limped for three steps, and straightened up.

"It's nothing," he said. "Caught the ball wrong, that's all."

"You sure?" asked Miriah. "That looked like it hurt."

"It was nothing," said Michael. He pulled at the ball with his left foot and dribbled the ball around a flat-footed Brandon. "See? Wanna try to catch me?"

"Had me worried for a moment," said Kyle. "Wouldn't want Michael hurt for the big game."

Ms. Wright blew a long blast on her whistle.

"Practice has officially begun," said Miriah.

The team gathered in a circle around Ms. Wright at the centre of the field.

"For the championship, we will be playing Grant Yeo Elementary," Ms. Wright said. "They are a good team. They also have two of Michael's old teammates from the Oshawa Kicks, so they will be a strong team."

"There goes the championship!" moaned Brandon, loudly.

"Suck it up, Sales," said Kyle.

"They have two strong players," said Miriah, "but we have a team."

Ms. Wright raised a hand. "But a team that has relied perhaps too much on Michael's talents. If we're going to have a chance Wednesday it has to be a full team effort. Now let's get out there. We're going to do some work on kicks: goal kicks, corner kicks, free kicks, penalty kicks — you name it. Let's do it!"

"I can't tell the difference," said Justin. "I just kick the ball every chance I get."

"Just follow what the seniors do," Ms. Wright said. "Watch

Michael and Brandon, Miriah and Alysha. They know what to do."

Michael exercised his damaged foot. He could dribble without problem. But any attempt to kick the ball with his right foot — his dominant right foot — sent a shaft of pain up his leg so strong it could have brought him to his knees. He hid this through the practice by making all his kicks with his left foot. He didn't want an injury to stop him from playing with either the Kicks or the school team.

When they worked on the corner kicks, Ms. Wright kept shaking her head. Finally, she blasted her whistle again and made circling motions with both hands, indicating they should gather around her.

"Those corner kicks aren't working well," she said. "Even on this smaller field, none of you can get it in front of the goal. Not even you, today, Michael. So we're going to practise playing short. On the full-size field on Wednesday, we'll have to do that."

They tried several more corner kicks, the forwards and midfielders in attacking positions. The backfielders took defensive positions to try to prevent scoring.

"Better, better, better," said Ms. Wright. "The backfield is looking great — nobody can score on them."

Michael gave one more try from the corner furthest from the school. The pass to the midfielders worked well, but Miriah lost possession before she could set up a scoring pass to Brandon.

Michael jogged to the front of the goal.

"Move that pass faster," he said to Miriah. "The other team won't give you any time on Wednesday."

"Duh," said Miriah. "Why don't we jump up and down with soccer spikes on each other?" she booted the ball at Michael.

Michael responded in sudden anger. He pulled back with his

good left foot and kicked the ball with all his might out of bounds.

"Oh, that's pretty," said Miriah, sarcastically. "Now, go fetch!"

The ball had crossed the field and rolled between two portable classrooms onto the paved area at the back of the school.

"Fetch it yourself," Michael replied sharply.

The rest of the team watched this exchange. They were stunned. From the other side of the portables, they could hear the ball bounce off the school wall and echo in smaller bounces until it meekly ended in silence.

"I'll get it," said Justin, his eyes sparkling.

But before he could move, they could hear the pronounced thump of a soccer ball being kicked. The ball came soaring through the air over the last portable and bounced twice in front of the goal.

"Whoa!" said Brandon. "Who did that?"

The team stood at centre field as though awaiting a visiting star. Mr. Rahilly appeared from between two portables.

"Have you finished up your football practice yet, Ms. Wright? " he said. "Or do you have time to look at one more draft choice?"

"Not Rahilly," said Brandon. "Who'd of thought he could kick a ball like that?"

"Go on! Haven't you heard that he played some pretty good soccer when he was a kid?"

"Hasn't everybody? Doesn't he go over that about once a month?"

"Draft choice?" Ms. Wright queried the other teacher. "Don't you think you're a bit old to try out for a soccer team like this, Mr. Rahilly? We're down to the last game of this spring season."

Mr. Rahilly walked across the field toward the coach.

"Oh, it's not for me," he said, his voice lilting even more than usual. "It's for someone else. I really think you should give this guy a look for Wednesday's game. I really do."

With a mild flourish, he pointed to the passage between two portables. Zahir emerged into the sunlight, looking to his left and right.

"Ms. Wright, would it be too late," Zahir said in his precise English way, "to try out for your football team?"

"Try out for our football team," repeated Ms. Wright.

"If it's not too late," Zahir said. "Mr. Rahilly thought I might have something to contribute."

Ms. Wright stood for a moment as though deep in thought.

"You have some positions that could use some bolstering," said Mr. Rahilly. "I have checked the rules, and there is nothing preventing his starting to play this late in the year."

Ms. Wright bit at her lower lip. "I wasn't thinking of that," she said. "I was thinking … oh, never mind. Zahir, what position do you play?"

Zahir took a few more steps out onto the field. "Please, Ms. Wright," he said. "On the last team I played I was centre forward. But in my home country … back in the camps … well, we paid no attention to positions. I could play anywhere I was needed, even goal." He hesitated for a moment and rested his foot on the soccer ball someone had rolled to him. "I was hoping to play. If I'm good enough. If I could fit into the team. If I would not displace anyone."

"If he's good enough," snorted Brandon, looking around at the team.

"He beat Cachuk at chess," said Justin at little more than a whisper.

"What's chess got to do with soccer, nim-nerf?" said Kyle.

"Well, no promises," said Ms. Wright, finally. "But you're welcome to work out with the team. Get some warm-up and we'll work you into our drills for today."

Zahir looked around the field. All eyes were on him. He looked up the field, where Erika stood in front of the goal. He moved the ball in front of him, starting upfield toward her.

Zahir handled the ball well. He dodged around Justin and Kyle, the ball close to his feet, his dark eyes darting around the field.

He twisted twice, turned once, and Michael watched as he came toward him. Michael swivelled and realized he was the only player between Zahir and the goal. He moved forward to cut off the newcomer.

"Undress him, Michael!" yelled Brandon.

Michael matched Zahir's movements step by step, chopping left when Zahir headed that way, turning back to the right as Zahir spun. Zahir kept the ball close to his feet but still loose enough to tempt Michael to rush in and pull it away.

Michael had played against too many good players to be fooled. Zahir could handle the ball well, and moved deceptively fast. Twisting, turning, the two players edged across the field, taking the play closer and closer to the goal. At a glance, Michael could see that Erika was moving back and forth in the goal mouth, ready for whatever came.

As they got closer to the goal, Zahir suddenly faked to the left and darted quickly to his right, sideways, in a final attempt to avoid the close checking Michael had provided. Michael followed, almost as fast.

But Zahir had begun the move, so he had a half-step start, kicking the ball ahead of him and sprinting hard. Michael followed, but Zahir pulled clear, tacked back to the left, and closed in on Erika in goal.

A full step now ahead of Michael, Zahir played the ball too long. Erika rushed forward and scooped up the ball, holding it aloft before punting it back down the field.

"Nice try," she said to Zahir with a smile.

"Good work," Zahir replied. He turned to Michael. "You play very well. You gave me some trouble there."

"Yeah, right," Michael mumbled grudgingly, thinking of the trouble he would like to provide.

Ms. Wright tooted her whistle again. "Okay, people," she said. "Back to your places. We're going to try those corner kicks again. That's one we've got to get right."

The team had been relying on Michael and Brandon for all corner kicks. If one took the kick, the other would plant himself firmly in a scoring position in front of the goal. Michael tried a few kicks. Limited to the use of his left foot, Michael's kicks lost both accuracy and power. All of his attempts fizzled and failed to reach the goal mouth, even on the shorter field. His attempts to pass short were inaccurate.

Brandon fared little better. He lacked the power to even attempt a long kick. His passes were woefully weak, easily intercepted, or both.

"Okay, Zahir."

The whistle tooted. Michael placed himself at the corner of the penalty area to the near side of the goal. Brandon pulled back behind him, ready to take the short pass. Michael tensed as Zahir kicked the ball.

The ball rocketed over Michael's head, goal-high, from a sharp, hard kick parallel to the goal line. It soared over Erika's outstretched hands, and curved toward the goal. It bounced off the inside of the far post and into the goal.

"Great kick!" Brandon said. "Wow! Did you see that? You see that, Michael? I've never seen anybody drop one like that.

Outside of the pros, that is. Did you see the way he bent that one in? It was stupendous!"

Michael shrugged.

Miriah ran in from midfield. "That was great, Zahir! Boy! Not even Michael can kick like that."

Michael watched as Zahir smiled shyly in answer to the praise. He was still thinking about it when he next kicked the ball, and did so with his right foot. He jogged across the field to work off the pain so no one would notice.

But everyone was watching Zahir, dribbling the soccer ball among, around, and through the rest of the team.

Michael had to admit that Zahir was good. Very, very good.

11

Michael is Jealous

Zahir joined Michael and Miriah in the library at noon.

"We really don't need to be doing this," said Michael. "Rahilly said the whole class was going to work on the report this afternoon."

"I just want to organize a bit," said Miriah. "We have most of the information we need. It's just a matter of how we present it."

"Well, you did a fine job in front of the school council, and look where it got us," said Michael.

Zahir sat on the edge of his chair as though he expected it to be pulled out from under him. "I don't mean to interfere with your discussion," he said. "My intent was not to get in your way." Michael could not get over the uppity-sounding accent in Zahir's voice.

"Well," Michael said, disdainfully, "Everybody keeps insisting that this is a team sport. What strengths do you bring to this team, Za-heer?" He pronounced the name with a mocking sharpness in the last syllable. "How can you help us?"

"Michael, don't be like that," said Miriah.

"Well," Zahir started. "I have lived through a war. In my home country of Afghanistan. And I am an orphan."

Miriah brightened. "You're from Afghanistan!" she said.

"Oh, you must have so much to tell!"

"You must have so much to tell!" sang Michael in a mocking voice. He found himself angry with Zahir and Miriah, and he didn't know why.

"Oh, yes," said Zahir. "As I was saying, in Afghanistan I lost my parents when I was very young."

"How? Bombs, or what?"

"In war, you lose count of the bombs and the explosions and who is fighting. I remember the noise and cold and hunger. And one day my parents were gone."

"That must have been awful," said Miriah. "You lost both parents? How old were you?"

"I don't remember. I remember the other children. Someone was always crying. And in the camp we played football. I wasn't very old."

"Football?" Michael asked.

"But how did you come here?" asked Miriah, ignoring Michael. "To Canada?"

Zahir's dark eyes sparkled at Michael. "Football. Soccer. We kicked at anything round." He turned to Miriah and answered, "From the camp I was adopted by Canadians. We lived in Britain, where they both worked, until earlier this year, when my father got a job in Canada."

"Your father?" asked Michael suspiciously.

"My adopted father," Zahir replied, without a pause. "He's a teacher. So's my mother. My adopted mother."

Michael slouched in his seat with his arms crossed. "Sounds like you lucked out," he said.

Miriah darted him a sharp look. "Don't be like that," she said.

"Many of my friends at the orphanage were not so lucky," Zahir said. "You have no idea …"

When Michael pushed back his chair he could feel the sharp pain along his shin. "I gotta join Brandon and Kyle and some others in the schoolyard," he said abruptly. "You're getting along fine here. You don't need me for anything more?"

"No, well, I guess … Yeah, we'll be okay," Miriah said, darting a glance at Zahir. "How are your ticket sales coming?"

"Ticket sales?" Michael replied.

"Michael, just because we still have to get official approval from the school council doesn't mean you can't sell tickets. Just not on school time."

"Yeah, right. Well … they're going okay," Michael said.

"You haven't started yet, have you? You took three books, and you haven't sold one ticket."

"I'll be out on the soccer field," Michael said. "They'll be sold. We've got a big game to get ready for. You'll be at practice tonight?"

"Whatever," Miriah replied.

12

A Good Report

Twice that afternoon in school, Michael avoided Zahir. The first time, during art class, Michael walked by his desk to pin his abstract landscape on the bulletin board in the hall.

"Michael," said Zahir, first checking to see that Mr. Rahilly was busy and would not notice. "It is important we—"

Michael didn't wait to hear more. He brushed by with a turn of his shoulders, pinching his still slightly wet painting by the edges using only his thumb and forefinger. He didn't need Zahir, didn't need the others either, if it came to that. He had agreed to help out the soccer team, that was all. If they didn't appreciate it, well, too bad.

He had trouble finding a vacant space on the bulletin board. No matter how he tried to fit his painting in place, it would end up covering part of someone else's painting.

"You find a spot?" asked Kyle, suddenly appearing beside him. "The board's not big enough. Here, try to fit your sheet in like this." Kyle slipped part of his painting behind one already pinned to the board, carefully overlapping his so the main area of the painting showed. "I ran into the same problem last week when Rahilly had me do the board at the back of the room," he said. "He explained something about the whole board then becoming a work of art."

"Yeah, sure," said Michael. His voice said he didn't believe any of it.

"You gonna be up for the big game?" Kyle asked. "I never thought we'd get this far."

"Yeah," said Michael. "With younger kids on the team. With the coach."

"You mean Ms. Wright?"

"And what's-his-name."

"Justin."

"Ms. Wright's coaching because last year nobody would. We wouldn't have had a team without her."

"She saddles you with that Little kid at every practice."

"Someone has to help kids like Justin. He's okay, you know."

"Don't tell him," Michael said, "or he'll be a real pain."

Kyle finished pinning his sheet in place and returned to the classroom. Michael struggled for a few minutes and then gave up. He took his sheet and pinned it dead centre on the board, covering the best part of three other paintings.

"There," he said, but there was no one to hear in the deserted hallway.

When the final bell sounded after school, Michael slipped out of the classroom first. He had to go by Zahir's desk, and so again heard the new student call his name.

"Michael …"

He ignored him. He shifted his backpack into place as he made his way down the corridor, aware that Zahir had followed him out of the classroom, but determined to pay no attention.

He would have escaped, would have been the first out of the school. But before Zahir could catch him and before he could make it to the door, he found his way blocked by the school principal.

"Michael," said Mrs. Moores. "I would like to see you and Miriah about your project."

"Project?"

"The written report for the school council. Do you have time now?"

"I …"

"Come with me."

The principal retreated into the office. She beckoned Michael inside. He was surprised to find Miriah already there, seated close to the front of the principal's desk.

"I thought you'd both like to know together," she said. "Your report has been accepted and the school council has approved your request for fundraising."

"You finished the report?" Michael said to Miriah.

"I said I would. Zahir helped me."

"Zahir? Can he even …?"

Mrs. Moores held up both hands. "I have no idea what you two are talking about, and I have a hunch I don't want to know. Whatever it is, focus on the good news. Mrs. Mitchell and a couple of others on her committee were in after lunch and read the report. Not only were they impressed, I was, too. It was very well structured and clear. You two have thought this through quite well. You are to be congratulated."

Michael exchanged glances with Miriah and shrugged. It wasn't his report.

"What does this mean?" asked Miriah.

"It means, for one thing, that your fundraising has an official charity number, since it is sanctioned and sponsored by the Parisotto school council. It means you can give the donors an official tax receipt. It also means that you must keep track of all the money raised and where it goes."

"You mean, we got it," said Miriah.

"You got it. We can talk about the details later. Right now it is enough to know that everything can go ahead. Congratulations."

Miriah thanked the principal. Michael left without saying a word. Miriah followed him into the foyer. "Thank goodness," she said. "I was worried. I didn't expect they'd decide so soon."

Michael didn't bother to look at her.

"So you can tell your friend that you can help all those orphans in Afghanistan," he said, his voice dripping with contempt. "Buy them a bunch of brand new soccer balls and make them feel real rich."

"Michael, what is the matter with you? I don't understand."

"What's to understand? You don't want my help. You don't *need* my help. Want me to repeat it?" Michael knew he was being unreasonable but couldn't stop the words.

"Michael Strike, you're being a jerk!"

Michael just walked away. Miriah didn't need him. He had been no help with the report. Even on the soccer field, everyone just watched the new kid. If they didn't need him, Michael thought, then why should he bother? Why should he play, even play through an injury, for the stupid school team when he had the Kicks team? He'd quit the Parisotto team, that's what.

Michael kept walking out the back door of the school onto the paved quadrangle. Past the portable classrooms he could see the deserted playground. The ground smelled of fresh rain.

By the big rock where the schoolyard became the park, Zahir was waiting for him.

13

Zahir Meets Michael

Zahir was leaning back on the rock, turning his face to the sun. Michael had been too deep in his own thoughts to see Zahir until it was too late to avoid him. Michael stopped about two metres away.

Zahir smiled. "Hello, Michael. I have been wanting to talk to you."

"Got no time," Michael replied. "Gotta go."

"Then I will walk with you," said Zahir, slipping from the rock and stepping in beside Michael. "I've seen you walk home every day. I live just down the street from you. So it is on my way home, too."

Michael hadn't known that. In the — what was it, two weeks? — that Zahir had been at the school, he had not noticed.

"We are neighbours," Zahir said, after a pause.

Michael looked at him sideways. He looked up and down the subdivision street. He wondered if it looked anything like the new kid's place in England. It must have seemed strange when compared to Afghanistan.

"So," Zahir said, matching his stride to Michael's, "You are a soccer star."

Michael glanced at him, not sure if he was being teased. "Well, you're good too," he replied grudgingly, admitting a truth he had been ignoring since practice the previous night.

Zahir nodded. "Thank you," he said. He shifted his backpack. "One thing I do not understand; why is it you do not like me?"

"Not like you?" Michael said, trying to sound surprised. But he knew he had been mean to Zahir and he didn't know why.

Zahir continued, "First you ignore me, and then all of a sudden you do not like me at all."

Michael looked at Zahir. He was still wearing the second-hand Blue Jays jacket. Why did that jacket bother Michael so much? It was clean, and had been in style once not long ago.

"Who says I don't like you?" Michael asked again. He turned a corner and headed up a sidewalk identical to the one he had been walking on. "Besides, is there a law that says I have to?"

Zahir fell in behind, hands in his jacket pockets. "I don't know anything about the law, but I just wondered. Is it something I have done, or said? Is it because I am new? Or where I'm from?"

Michael stopped and looked at Zahir.

"All that's got nothing to do with anything."

Zahir shrugged. Michael was surprised to see it was a very Canadian shrug. "Everybody laughed at me that first day in school. I don't know why. Everyone likes you. I was hoping you could tell me what I did wrong."

They kept walking, this time side by side.

"That was Brandon," Michael said at last. "The laughing." Michael cringed inside as he recalled the day the class laughed when *his* voice broke.

"But everybody laughed. All but Miriah. I could be her friend."

"You are Miriah's friend. You two did a great job on that report."

"You saw it?"

"Mrs. Moores just told us that the raffle's been approved. The report did it." He walked on, his brain reaching for the connection. Then he stopped. "It's the jacket."

Zahir looked at his sleeve. "The jacket?"

"I had a jacket like that last year. *Just* like that. I gave it to the Salvation Army to give to poor people. It's an old jacket."

Zahir looked from his sleeve to Michael and back. "I still don't understand. It is a very good jacket. The Blue Jays are my favourite team."

"It's the crest."

"The crest?" said Zahir, with a puzzled look.

"Yes. The Blue Jays logo, there." He pointed to the colourful emblem. "That's the old logo. The Blue Jays changed it. Everybody got the new jacket, with the new crest. That's why I gave mine away."

Zahir examined the logo on his jacket. He brushed at the sleeve.

"You mean," he said, "you gave away a jacket because the picture on it wasn't new anymore?"

Michael chewed on his lip and looked thoughtful. "When you put it that way," he said, "it sounds stupid, doesn't it?"

"My parents didn't know that the crest had changed." Zahir sounded baffled, as though he had discovered that even his own new parents did not fully understand their own culture.

"My father said it was very Canadian," Zahir explained. "And so I like wearing it, even though it is not new. And you must have liked it once, if it belonged to you."

Michael looked at Zahir and saw he was serious. "Naw, Brandon was just making a joke. I had told about giving my old jacket to the clothing drive because I wanted to impress Miriah. She was starting that war orphans thing then."

"This isn't your jacket, then?"

"Not in a million years."

"But it has your name in the back. Look." Zahir slipped out of his backpack and pulled the back of his collar out to reveal the label. Smeared in ballpoint ink was the name: *Michael S.*

Michael looked at in disbelief.

"It really is!" he said. "Where did you get it?"

Zahir put his backpack back on. "When we came from England last month we helped neighbours take some clothes to the place — what do you call it?"

"Salvation Army."

"Yes. I saw this jacket. My father likes baseball and I have become a Blue Jays fan. So we bought it."

Michael recalled his last Blue Jays game. His father had tickets for a corporate box. There was plenty to eat and drink, but his father spent the time talking to clients. The game was a long way away down on the field. He couldn't see very well.

Michael smiled. "How'd you meet your parents?" he asked. "Them being Canadian and all, and you in Afghanistan."

Zahir pointed to a house diagonally across from the corner from where they stood. "That's my house," he said. "You want to come in?" When Michael made no sign of moving, Zahir went on. "My birth parents were killed when a land mine blew up on the road, one left over from another war with the Russians. I was in an orphanage when the bombs fell in the latest war. My new parents had come over to help, and that's where they found me."

"But you speak English pretty good."

"We lived in England for two years."

"That's where you get the English accent. It surprised me. Surprised everybody."

"And my birth parents spoke English, I am told, even

though it was forbidden. They would be glad to know I am not living in Afghanistan. But someday I will go back. In the orphanage there were so many of my friends that had only each other. I promised them I would go back and try to help them."

Michael looked Zahir in the eye. "We each help," he said, remembering what Kyle had said. "I'm sorry for giving you a hard time. It wasn't nice. I didn't make you feel welcome."

"It is no problem." Mixed in with Zahir's British accent, Michael could hear other traces from another land.

"Hey, you play chess. Cachuk's a strong player. You beat him."

"We had a tough battle," said Zahir.

"Yeah, but you beat him, man! I've never been able to do that."

"It was luck."

"Yeah, luck in chess. Just the roll of the pieces, eh?" Michael gave Zahir a friendly jab on the arm. "And you play soccer real good, too," Michael said, in the awkward pause that followed. "That surprised me. I'm glad Ms. Wright decided you could play tomorrow."

"At the orphanage we used to play with a old ball that didn't have all the air in it. We stuffed it with old rags. In England I played. Only there, they call it football."

Michael smiled. "But here football is three downs and passing. Want to hear something funny? My granddad calls Canadian football rugby."

"In England that is a different game with a ball that is rounder at the ends."

"Confusing, eh? But we just play plain soccer."

Zahir said, "In England they call it Association football. That's the official term. Association football." He paused, then asked, "How did you hurt your foot?"

Michael turned to him, surprised. "What do you mean?" He had told no one about his foot, not even his parents. The first league game with the Kicks was a week away.

"You have hurt your kicking foot. I watched you at practice. You could dribble and kick very well with your left foot. But not with your right foot."

Michael turned away. "I didn't think anybody would notice."

"Should you rest it?"

"You mean not play in the championship game? There's not much choice left," he said. "If there are two guys from the Kicks on the Grant Yeo team, then we're going to need all the help we can get. If I sat out with a sore foot, they'd be all over us."

"You would risk a season of soccer for this one game?"

Michael thought about the question. Finally, he said, "For the championship? Yesterday I would have said no. But it's important to a lot of others. Even my parents said they would be at the school board meeting trying to keep our school open. The meeting's the same time as our game. It'd help if we won the championship."

"Soccer would keep a school open?"

"Not soccer itself. But Dad says it would draw more attention to the school and make it harder for the board to close it."

"It is important then."

"More important to us at Tarcisio Parisotto Elementary School than to anybody at Yeo Elementary. More to me and my friends than to those other guys from the Kicks."

"You know these players?" Zahir asked.

"I don't know which ones they are," said Michael. "When I see them, I'll know them. But if they were on the Kicks, they'll be good and hard to stop."

"But you can stop them? Enough to give the goalie —

Erika? — a good chance. She's a good player."

"She has improved," agreed Michael. He remembered that first practice and how frightened she had been.

"She shows no fear," said Zahir. "She will do well against this other team."

"They won't be easy," said Michael. "I wasn't the best player on the Kicks. Whoever they are, they'll be tough."

"I will help where I can."

"We'll need to work together."

Zahir smiled widely. "We will be teammates," he said.

"Teammates," replied Michael, and he and Zahir grinned at each other.

They stood on the sidewalk in an awkward silence. Then Zahir spoke.

"Miriah." He said just the one word.

"Yeah," said Michael. "You and she did a good job on that report. Miriah can sell tickets and everything."

"I'm glad it turned out well," said Zahir.

"You must have studied well. Mrs. Moores said the report was great." He paused for a moment. "This whole thing about war orphans was Miriah's idea. She likes to organize stuff."

"Miriah — is she your girlfriend?" Zahir asked. "Are you angry I worked on the report with her? I helped her rewrite it so it told more about the orphans in Afghanistan."

"You did a good job," Michael repeated.

"If it raises some money for my orphanage back in Afghanistan, and helps my friends back there, then I'll be happy."

"You could send them my old jacket."

Zahir looked at the Blue Jays jacket and laughed. "It would be much better to send money that will help people rebuild. So is she? Your girlfriend?"

Michael looked at Zahir. "I wanted to impress her," he said. "Now, the only thing that would do that would be if I sell all these tickets she gave me. Hey! Maybe you could help me."

"I will help you if I can. We are teammates. And friends?"

"Friends, yes. And teammates. Can you help me sell them this afternoon?" Michael asked.

"I have two books, too! Miriah gave them to me. She is very persistent," Zahir said. "Well, you know this neighbourhood, and I know about war orphans, so we could try together."

"Yeah, together," Michael said, as though he had not thought of that. "We could go over to the plaza and, like, hit all the merchants, ask if we can approach customers. Go up and down this street. What do you say?"

Zahir turned into his driveway. "I must ask my parents first," he said. "Come on in. And I will help you, right?"

"Right."

Zahir smiled. "In my old country we have a saying," he said. "'A real friend is one who takes the hand of his friend in times of distress and helplessness.'"

Michael put his hand on his new friend's shoulder. "I wouldn't say I'm exactly helpless," he said, "but maybe I was in some distress."

14

Vasco's Field

When the soccer team from Tarcisio Parisotto Elementary School emerged from the schoolbus at the University of Ontario, they were awe-struck.

The game was being played on Vasco's Field. Both the field and the university were new, situated in the north end of Oshawa. Vasco's Field was named after Vasco Vujanovic, soccer coach of the Durham College Lords for many years. The field was built in a pasture converted from Windfield Farms, home of some of the world's best race horses.

"Wow!" said Brandon. "This is the best soccer field I've ever seen."

Michael was impressed but tried not to show it. "It's a soccer field," he said. "It's got lines in the right places and a goal at each end. What more's to know?"

"But look at the lights!" said Kyle. "I'll bet at night this is as bright as day!"

Miriah looked at him. "But it is daytime now," she said. "Which makes it bright as day. The lights only count if you use them."

"And the dome!" said Brandon. "Look at the dome! I'll bet it's big enough to play tennis in. That's awesome!"

"That *is* for tennis," said Miriah.

"Do you play tennis?" asked Zahir.

"Well, no," replied Brandon, almost sheepishly. "But I bet it's big enough. It's bigger than the dome at Civic, and that one has three tennis courts."

"Look, there's the Grant Yeo team!" said Erika, adjusting her yellow bandana to hold her ponytail out of the way.

Michael looked out on the field. Several members of the Yeo team, dressed in bright yellow sweaters, were already warming up on the field. He scanned the players and right away focused on two of them.

"It's Armana and Klucker," he said.

"What's that?" asked Zahir, the only one close enough to hear.

"The two Kicks players. Bruce Armana and Dan Klucker. They're both good scorers. We could be in trouble."

"What?" asked Brandon, as they approached the edge of the field.

"Pass it to me," said Justin. "I'll score."

"Yeah, kid, right," said Brandon. "Have you touched the ball all season?"

"Time for the warm-up," said Ms. Wright, dumping a bag-ful of balls onto the field. "Just limber up."

"Armana and Klucker," repeated Michael to Brandon. Some of the other players gathered around.

"What is it?" asked Erika. "Those two? Are we supposed to be intimidated?"

"We'll see how you feel when they boot one at you full in the face," said Brandon.

Michael took a soccer ball and jogged onto the field, drib-bling. Near the centre of the field, Bruce Armana approached to retrieve a ball.

"This is going to be a blow-out, Strike," he said. "We've got you outnumbered."

"What? Outnumbered? You're only allowed eleven on the field, same as us."

Armana, who was thin and wiry, laughed. "You know what I mean, Strike. There's one of you and two of us: me and Klucker. We make a great team. Last game we won by a score of twelve to nothing."

"It's a good thing there's two of you," replied Michael. "That should even the odds." It was an empty boast, but Michael found that it made him feel more hopeful about the game.

Back at the bench, Ms. Wright gave the players their last-minute instructions.

"Remember, you played hard to get here," she said. "Just get out there and do your best."

"Zahir and I will watch them," Michael said.

"Pardon?" asked Ms. Wright. "Who?"

Michael filled Ms. Wright in on Armana and Klucker. "They're good, and there's two of them. They'll dominate the play. If Zahir and I stick to them we can keep them from running away with the game."

Ms. Wright looked dubious. "Well, okay. We'll put in match-up positions. Work it out when you get out there."

The referee blew one long blast on his whistle. The teams took their positions. The game was on.

* * *

Grant Yeo Elementary kicked off to start the game. Bruce Armana took the ball and launched it over the heads of the forwards.

It was not a particularly good kick. Michael knew Armana could do better, could kick further. He turned and watched the ball hang in the air before dropping among the midfielders.

As he watched, he felt rather than saw Armana and both his forwards race past, headed for the ball. Too late, Michael saw what should have been obvious: the high lobbed ball give the Yeo forwards time to challenge the Parisotto midfield.

Facing his own goal, he glanced off to the right. Zahir ran smoothly between Dan Klucker and the ball. Ahead, Armana arrived in the middle of the midfielders as the ball came down. Deftly, he took the ball on his chest. As he ran, he let the ball roll to his feet.

Miriah stepped in front of him. Armana moved left, then right, turning a complete circle to avoid Kyle coming in from the left. He easily eluded both, and continued to the Parisotto goal.

Now Michael was on his heels, the shadow he should have been from the kickoff. Between Armana and Erika in goal, two backfielders formed a mini wall. Michael knew Armana could dribble around them easily. But that would allow Michael to overtake his opponent.

To his right, Michael caught a glimpse of Klucker racing in, all speed and power — with nothing between him and Erika. Armana saw him too, and kicked a rolling ball into the penalty zone to feed him. A free and clear kick at goal — with Erika out of position.

Before Klucker could take the ball, Zahir pulled between Klucker and the perfect pass. Zahir took control of the ball. Pursued now by Klucker, he rolled it to Erika, who grabbed it in both hands and punted it downfield.

"Way to go!" Michael said to Zahir.

"We are like glue," Zahir replied.

Michael stuck even closer to Armana. When Armana raced downfield, Michael stayed with him, stride for stride. Always placing himself between his opponent and the ball, Michael struggled to prevent him from creating another scoring opportunity.

On the right side of the field, Zahir did the same with Klucker. Up and down the field they ran. During a throw-in in the first half, Michael saw Klucker and Armana exchange words. From that point on, both Yeo players ignored their positional play, criss-crossing the field almost randomly.

Armana tried many tricks. First he would roar toward the ball, pulling Michael with him. Then he would dart away, heading for an open wing and the hopes of a pass. He darted left; Michael covered. He darted right; Michael moved with him.

Only once did Armana's tactics work.

Armana faked a move toward centre field, where his centre midfielder held the ball at his feet, looking for a pass. Michael covered the move, placing himself between Armana and the ball carrier.

In an instant Armana reversed direction. The pass lobbed over Michael's head, dropping at Armana's feet.

Michael said something his grandmother would have frowned on and grunted after Armana. Michael's pursuit left the other player no time. A hurried pass missed its mark. Justin raced to it, picking up the loose ball at the top of the penalty area.

"Boot it! Boot it!" cried Erika from the goal.

Panicked by thundering forwards coming at him from both sides, Justin attempted to dribble forward. He got nowhere. A midfielder from the Yeo team raced in, took the ball close to his feet and kicked it free.

A Yeo forward cut in from the left and took the loose ball under control. In two steps he booted hard and high. A flying Erika came out of nowhere and palmed the ball off its path, deflecting it off the inside corner of the goalpost — and in the goal.

The score: 1–0 for Yeo Elementary.

"That's okay," Michael whispered to Justin, who was making faces and kicking at the grass.

"I let him through," Justin said.

"Don't worry. We'll get it back. But don't try to dribble in your own end. Get it, boot it. We'll be okay."

"Yeah," the younger player said, unconvinced.

"Nice try, Erika," said Zahir. "They were just lucky on that one."

"Don't sweat it," Michael added.

A few minutes later, Michael broke free of Armana to pick up a loose ball near the Yeo goal. His hurried kick sent the ball toward the far corner. The goalie batted the ball free, knocking it into the end zone over the goal line.

"Corner kick," signalled the referee, pointing to the corner flag.

Michael took the kick. Zahir tried to position himself in front of the goal. But having Michael make the kick left both Klucker and Armana to cover Zahir.

Michael kicked, trying to avoid both defenders, and so was not able to get the ball to Zahir. Instead, he lofted it high into the penalty area. Miriah headed the pass in the direction of Zahir. Armana swept in and took control of the ball, dribbling almost the whole length of the field before Zahir caught him.

When the whistle sounded to end the first half, the score was still 1–0.

15

The Corner Kick

Nice work out there, people," said Ms. Wright. "We'll get 'em in the second half."

"Sorry about letting that one in," said Erika.

"That was not your fault," said Ms. Wright. "That was a good try. Justin, don't be down on yourself about that. And everyone remember: you get the ball in your own end, just kick it clear."

"Every time?" asked Justin.

"Every time. I know it is difficult when you have ten big kids running at you. Just get it clear."

"Yeah, just don't get in the road, kid," said Kyle. "I don't wanna trip over you out there." He rubbed the top of Justin's head.

"Your own big feet'll do that for you," said Justin, smiling.

Mr. Rahilly came over from the sidelines. He had been standing with the few parents who had not gone to the school board committee meeting.

Michael's parents had promised to be at the meeting. At noon, his father called to say he was tied up with clients. His mother promised to cut short her workout to be there. Michael wondered if she did.

"Your team is doing well, Ms. Wright," Mr. Rahilly said.

"You have some younger players, but the team is right into the game."

"They know what they have to do."

"May I speak to a couple of your players?" he asked. "About a small observation I've made?"

Ms. Wright nodded. Mr. Rahilly gave a sideways nod of his head toward Michael and Zahir. The two joined the coach and the Irish teacher.

"You're doing a good job, you two," he said. "But a heads-up about those two Yeo superstars." His accent slathered on the sarcasm.

"What's that?" asked Michael.

"That big guy, what's his name?"

"Klucker."

"Right. If it comes to a choice between him and the smaller guy, cover Armana. Klucker couldn't shoot holes in a ladder."

"He's strong."

"Yes, he's got a long boot but he doesn't know where it's ending up at. Armana now — he'd steal the sugar out of your punch."

"What does that mean?" said Brandon, who had joined them. "What's he talking about?"

Zahir turned to him. "He said that Klucker has a strong kick but can't aim it. Armana, on the other hand, is a very good ball handler."

"When did you learn to speak Irish?" asked Miriah.

"In England," Zahir replied, "two of my mates were Irish."

Michael turned to Zahir. "Armana is getting away from me the odd time. Think you could keep up with him?"

"No problem," replied Zahir. "He is faster than Klucker, but not so fast that I can't keep up. I would not want him making a good kick on goal."

"Want to trade?" Michael asked. "You cover Armana and I'll stick to Klucker."

It was Zahir's turn to pause. "I could use my speed to shadow him," he said. "That would work."

From anyone else this might seem a boast. Michael remembered that first day in practice when Brandon had commented on his skills.

"Don't be bragging now, Zahir," said Brandon.

Michael looked at him. "If you can do it, it's not bragging," he said. "And Zahir can do it."

The referee tooted the whistle. They were ready to start the second half.

Ms. Wright pointed first at Michael and then at Zahir. "You two," she said. "Forget anything about positions. Just shadow those two wherever they go."

"Right," said Michael. "Now here's the plan ..."

* * *

Michael took the kickoff to start the second half.

Opposite him, Armana stared him down, daring him to open up the game. This time, however, Michael booted the kickoff long and deep, and raced past Armana to pursue it.

The Grant Yeo team backfielder was surprised when Michael confronted her before she had the ball under control. She tried to pass across, but her backfield partner was not ready either, and fumbled the ball before he could boot it out of the zone.

Michael snapped up the loose ball, deked once around the startled backfielder, and closed in on the goal.

He could see the focus in the goalkeeper's eyes. He touched the ball, positioning it two metres ahead, and raced to it. He drew back his right foot and aimed a heavy kick to the top left corner.

He caught the ball with his instep. A sweet *thunk* came from the ball as it soared toward the open top left corner of the goal.

Pain shot up his leg: a numbing, shocking, sharp, searing pain. He rolled to the grass, deaf to the cheers of his teammates as the ball settled into the mesh netting in the goal.

The score was tied: 1–1.

Michael got back to his feet, limping for a few paces on the trampled sod.

"Are you okay, Michael?" asked Miriah, rushing over.

"What happened?" asked Brandon.

"That was a pretty goal," said Zahir, kneeling beside him. "Your sore foot?"

"I'm fine now," Michael said. "Really, I am." His limp had now disappeared. "See?" He could no longer feel the pain — only where the pain had been.

"Are you sure you should play?" asked Miriah. "It's not the end of the world, you know."

"It's important to too many people," said Michael. "Let's do it."

Armana took the return kickoff, playing the ball high and deep. Both he and Klucker rushed in, hoping to panic the back-fielders before they had gained control — just as Michael had started the half.

Zahir not only picked up Armana, he got in front of him, carefully keeping between him and the ball. Klucker spied Zahir and closed in on him, not yet aware that Michael and Zahir had swapped roles. For one confusing minute, Klucker tried to check Zahir, Zahir tried to keep close to Armana, and Michael shadowed Klucker. They bunched on the field like pre-schoolers.

The ball squirted out of the scrum to Kyle, who booted it out of the zone. Miriah picked it up along the sideline. She headed downfield at full stride, a midfielder in attacking mode.

Michael exchanged glances with Zahir. Zahir followed behind Miriah, back ten metres and a few metres off the sideline. Michael headed for the front of the goal, ready for any pass.

Miriah kicked the ball across field. Michael looked back. Armana was clinging to Zahir. Klucker hadn't clued in quite so fast. Undecided about which opponent he should shadow on this attack, he took the middle ground, placing himself half-way between Zahir and Michael, which meant he covered nobody. This left Michael in the clear.

Miriah's pass came wobbly over to the top of the Yeo penalty area. Michael headed it once, to his left, back to Miriah. He could see Miriah race from the corner in time to pick up the pass.

She kicked once from a sharp angle. Michael winced as he heard the ball glance off the far goalpost — and out again.

The ball rolled parallel to the goal line. Michael headed sharply for it, clear now in a perfect scoring chance. Even from this sharp angle, he thought, he could make it.

He met the ball as he leaned to his left, the ball teed up perfectly for his kicking foot. His right kicking foot. He remembered the pain. He checked his pace, tried to shift his position to set up the ball to kick with his left foot. The extra movement cost him a precious split-second. Two backfielders were on him then, and before he could move around them the goalkeeper had moved back into position. Klucker thundered in like a freight train.

"Sorry," he mouthed to Miriah as the play shifted upfield.

"Next time," she mouthed back.

Michael attached himself to Klucker. The bigger boy was

not as fast as Armana, did not turn as quickly. More important, Michael concluded, was that he did not anticipate the play as well as his teammate. He was, though, still an excellent player, and Michael knew he could be dangerous in many situations.

Exactly how dangerous, he found out as the clock on the game wound down. Kyle had picked up the ball just inside mid-field. He booted the ball as hard as he could. Michael turned on the sound of the kick, racing downfield on the attack.

The ball bounced once off a defending Yeo player and headed back toward the Parisotto goal. Michael turned, but saw too late that his anticipation had allowed Klucker between him and the ball.

Michael sprinted back, but Klucker had possession and was on his way. He was a lumbering hulk of a guy. He pushed the ball ahead and ran full tilt after it. His dribbling was neither pre-cise nor pretty, but it was effective, since it allowed him to motor at full speed.

Michael gained on him, but not enough. Twice Klucker kicked the ball ahead, caught it, kicked it ahead, as the ball rolled inside the penalty area. Between the ball and the goal only one player remained: Erika. She stood her ground in the goal area, poised and ready.

Klucker focused on the ball and roared in. Michael charged in from behind, two metres back. He saw Klucker draw his foot back. He could see the fear in Erika's eyes, but she did not flinch as Klucker kicked.

Erika had advanced far enough out of the goal to cut down the angles, minimizing the amount of net Klucker could see. He aimed for the top right corner, a rocket of a shot. Erika flew in the air, catching the edge of the ball with her outstretched hand just enough to deflect the ball off target, so it missed the goal-post by a finger.

The referee signalled: corner kick.

Both sides knew they were in the dying minutes of the game. A goal now would clinch the game, the championship.

Klucker took the corner kick just as expected.

Zahir moved like a shadow, inserting himself between Armana and the kicker. He moved with Armana almost like a second skin. If Armana moved back, Zahir was there. If he jogged in, Zahir was there.

Michael sized up the situation quickly. With Klucker taking the kick, and Armana covered, that left Michael free to cover any free attacker, or, if the opportunity arose, to grab a loose ball. He planted himself on the penalty line, three metres out from the goal.

Predictably, Klucker used his power in the kick. The ball rose high and came in short of the goal, but not by much. Michael saw that Klucker could not make it into the play in time, and took the ball on his chest.

Immediately he was surrounded and pinned in. Deftly, he deked back, rolling the ball to his own goal.

Erika scooped up the ball. Michael had already turned and began sprinting straight downfield. Behind him he knew Erika had the ball, was running with it. *Thunk!* He could hear the punt. He looked over his shoulder to see the ball soaring over his head. It bounced twice in front of him before he caught it.

Three backfielders had fallen back to prevent just such a break. Michael could see them scramble. Klucker was well back, and even the midfielders for the Yeo team, had they been in position, could not have caught him. He had plenty of room to run.

The first backfielder made the mistake of trying to look backward while running toward his own goal. He twisted, and as he did Michael went around him on the other side. Trying to recover, he went down like a pretzel.

The last two defenders had spread themselves too thin. Rather than pair together to force Michael to beat them both at the same time, they had separated, perhaps fearing a pass. Michael deked around the first, turned suddenly to avoid the second, and closed in on the goal.

But trying to adjust to his left kicking foot threw his timing. He slowed half a pace. Defenders were on his back. Hurried, he kicked hard. He watched as the goalie cringed, the ball bouncing off his forearms, which he held like a shield before his face.

Michael missed the rebound. A charging backfielder caught the loose ball and booted it hard into the end zone, ending any hope of a second try.

The referee tooted the play: corner kick, Parisotto.

The game was in its last minute. The Grant Yeo team called a time out.

16

The Rahilly Cup

The Parisotto team huddled before the goal.

"You take the kick," Zahir said.

"You have to take it," Michael said, indicating his injured foot with his eyes in a way he was sure no one but Zahir would understand. "You've got the heavy foot. And they won't be expecting it."

"What's the matter?" asked Brandon. "No way. Mike, get in there and boot it."

"Give it to me," said Justin. "I'll score."

"Yeah, right, kid," said Kyle. "Just don't get in anybody's way."

"Zahir's going to take the corner kick," Michael said, addressing the whole team. "We all know what to do."

"Got it," the team said in unison, but Brandon's eyes said he wasn't sure.

The referee sounded the whistle to restart the action.

At the corner, Zahir stood two paces back from the ball. Michael worked to find a position in front of the goal. Armana twisted back and forth in front of him, covering him closely. Klucker had planted himself at the top of the goal area, ready to pounce on a loose ball — and to cover Zahir when he rushed to get into the action.

Michael nodded once to Miriah, to his right. The whistle sounded.

Zahir caught the ball squarely. It rose in a climbing arch toward the goal.

Both teams jostled on the near side of the goal, expecting a direct kick to fall short. But instead of aiming the kick close to the front of the goal, Zahir's kick curved away from the goal — directly to Miriah at the top of the penalty area. The defenders surged forward to cover her. Quickly, she passed back to Zahir, who was now charging toward the goal, uncovered.

Michael saw his opportunity: open space between him and the goal.

Zahir dribbled toward the goal, eluding first one defender, then another, drawing defenders in a crush toward him. Michael watched transfixed as Zahir worked within striking distance.

One step, two steps, three.

Klucker appeared out of nowhere, a lurking hulk of an obstacle that somehow defied gravity. Zahir dodged; Klucker clung. Zahir deked; Klucker still clung. Between Zahir and the goal there was now no space.

Zahir spied Michael through the maze. He chipped the ball aloft, not a hard pass — soft, really — but it had only one place to go. Michael was in the air to intercept, heading the ball sharply toward the goal. He watched the ball floating toward the open side of the goal.

The Yeo goalie had leaped into the air to stop Zahir's kick. Michael's header caught him coming down when he should have been going up, but somehow he batted the ball away with one hand anyway.

Michael landed on his side with a grunt. He watched as the ball bounced — once, twice — rolling as though in slow motion, dwindling in smaller bounces.

The Yeo goalie landed heavily beside him. The ball rolled along the goal line, heading past the far post and heading meekly out of bounds.

The field, the game, froze in time. The ball bounced away, forever out of reach. Shouts reached him as though from a far-away field.

A small bundle of elbows and knees moved frame by frame from the left. Justin, the fifth grader who everyone forgot, came pounding in, his face twisted in effort, his mouth open for a scream that Michael could not hear.

Inch by inch, the ball bounced away; inch by inch, Justin strained toward it, a small boy in a molasses world.

Step, bounce, step, bounce, like a slow-motion dance in a bad dream.

The players, coaches, teachers, parents — everyone sucked in a breath, swallowed sound.

The ball dribbled by the far post.

Justin caught it then. It wasn't much of a kick. It didn't need to be. The angle was sharp. Justin touched the ball with his left foot. It reversed direction, skidded by the post, and headed back toward the goal. It rolled and rolled along the goal line, and rolled and rolled some more, and suddenly it was in — over the line for the winning goal.

A shout exploded across the field and sideline at once.

Justin started his victory shout as he kicked, both hands straight into the air, eyes dancing in devilish delight.

The referee blew a long, double blast on the whistle. The game was over.

Justin's teammates descended in a mob. Kyle grabbed his small teammate around the waist and lifted him to his shoulders. At full gallop, he circled the field, his teammates in pursuit.

At the bench, Brandon and Michael lifted Ms. Wright onto their shoulders.

"Careful, now, boys," said Mr. Rahilly. "She'll only bounce in one direction."

Players, parents, and coach hugged and yelled and high-fived until their hands smarted. They were delirious. Tarcisio Parisotto was city soccer champion!

Afterward, Armana and Klucker shook hands with every-one.

"Great game," Armana said to Michael. "You out for the Kicks game next week?"

"Wouldn't miss it," Michael said, hoping his foot would approve.

"Bring your buddy," said Armana, pointing to Zahir. "He'd fit in well. The Kicks sure could use a guy like him."

"Hear that, Zahir?"

"I will try out for the team," said Zahir. "Can I wear my Blue Jays jacket?"

* * *

The next morning, Miriah walked to the front of the room before class began. "Does everyone have their War Orphans tickets sold? Today's the last day. Hand in your books."

She looked at Michael impatiently. "Nudge, nudge," she said. "Even if you haven't sold any, hand in the books. Alysha sold all four of hers."

"Just four?" asked Brandon, sarcastically.

"How about you, Michael?" asked Miriah. "Have you even *started* yet?"

"As matter of fact," said Michael, "I have."

"A book?"

"All of them," Michael replied.

"All three?" Miriah replied, unbelieving.

Zahir entered the classroom smiling.

"All of them," said Michael, as he placed on her desk a locked plastic bag jingling with change and showing several bills. "Five."

"Five? Michael? You had only three books to begin with!"

"Five. But not just me," Michael replied. "Zahir and me. We worked together. We sold my three books and his two. Is that enough? We can sell more if there's more time."

"We did it as a team," Zahir said. "Once around the whole plaza, every business and every customer. And our neighbours."

"We told them it was for Zahir's old orphanage," Michael said, "in Afghanistan. That's okay, isn't it? We were going to bring it up in class. Rather than just have this drive for War Orphans of the World, you know, without a real target. Zahir knows what is needed."

Miriah looked at the pair. "You two make a good team," she said.

Mr. Rahilly and Ms. Wright entered the room. They carried a huge trophy, with a big rounded cup and several blank tags around the base.

"Ladies and gentlemen," he said, "may I introduce you to the Rahilly Cup."

"The Rahilly Cup?" asked Brandon.

The teacher grinned. "I was dismayed to discover that the city school soccer championship has no trophy. Well, having a certain love of the game me ownself, I decided that could not be. So I went out and bought this trophy, and will present it. The board has already accepted it as an annual trophy."

"Why'd you do that?" asked Kyle.

"Pay back, lad, pay back. When I came to this country, I

was so poor I had forty-five ways of getting into my jacket. I didn't get to play soccer here. This is my way of leaving a mark."

"There are no names on it."

"We have to send it out for engraving. I just picked it up last night."

The bell sounded.

"Places, everyone," said Mr. Rahilly. "You may be soccer champions, but this class has got work to do."

"And war orphans to support," said Kyle.

Ms. Wright nodded. "That's been a great project," she said. "You guys have proven that a small school can still do some great things."

"And you, Ms. Wright. This trophy proves that championship teams are created by coaches," said Mr. Rahilly. "Thanks to you, this school had a soccer team. You made it happen."

"Yes, thanks," said Erika. "We all appreciate what you've done."

Mr. Rahilly rubbed his hands together. "But first, right after opening exercises, I want all the soccer players out in the lobby. We have some pictures to take of a certain soccer team. And don't you be running off now, Ms. Wright. Mrs. Moores said she would look after your class. And you, Kyle; run down to the Grade Five class and get Justin and Victoria. Don't stand here breathing! Get moving!"

"What about you, Mr. Rahilly?" asked Brandon. "Won't you be in the photo?"

"I wasn't involved. Not this time. Besides, somebody's got to snap the birdie."

"But would you be involved?" asked Ms. Wright. "Next year I certainly could use some help."

"We don't know that the school will be open next year, do we?" said Mr. Rahilly.

"Well," said Miriah, "my mother said the school board did listen to the parents yesterday. No decision has been made. Which means we've still got work to do."

"Oh, no," said Brandon. "Miriah's getting wound up again. What part of the world are you going to save now?"

"Not the world, Miriah replied. "This school. We need to take these last ten days of school and do what we can to stop the closing of Tarcisio Parisotto Elementary."

Michael laughed. "What about it, Mr. Rahilly? Could we end the year with a project in civics class?"

Mr. Rahilly smiled. "There's little time, but it's not a completely daft idea. But first, let's go get these pictures taken. Let's take this one victory at a time."

Other books you'll enjoy in the Sports Stories series

Baseball

❏ *Curve Ball* by John Danakas #1
Tom Poulos is looking forward to a summer of baseball in Toronto until his mother puts him on a plane to Winnipeg.

❏ *Baseball Crazy* by Martyn Godfrey #10
Rob Carter wins an all-expenses-paid chance to be bat boy at the Blue Jays spring training camp in Florida.

❏ *Shark Attack* by Judi Peers #25
The East City Sharks have a good chance of winning the county championship until their arch rivals get a tough new pitcher.

❏ *Hit and Run* by Dawn Hunter and Karen Hunter #35
Glen Thomson is a talented pitcher, but as his ego inflates, team morale plummets. Will he learn from being benched for losing his temper?

❏ *Power Hitter* by C. A. Forsyth #41
Connor's summer was looking like a write-off. That is, until he discovered his secret talent.

❏ *Sayonara, Sharks* by Judi Peers #48
In this sequel to *Shark Attact*, Ben and Kate are excited about the school trip to Japan, but Matt's not sure he wants to go.

❏ *Out of Bounds* by Sylvia Gunnery # 70
When the Hirtle family's house burns down, Jay is forced to relocate and switch schools. He has a choice: sacrifice a year of basketball or play on the same team as his arch-rival Mike.

Basketball

❏ *Fast Break* by Michael Coldwell #8
Moving from Toronto to small-town Nova Scotia was rough, but when Jeff makes the school basketball team he thinks things are looking up.

❏ *Camp All-Star* by Michael Coldwell #12
In this insider's view of a basketball camp, Jeff Lang encounters some unexpected challenges.

❏ *Nothing but Net* by Michael Coldwell #18
The Cape Breton Grizzly Bears prepare for an out-of-town basketball tournament they're sure to lose.

❏ *Slam Dunk* by Steven Barwin and Gabriel David Tick #23
In this sequel to *Roller Hockey Blues*, Mason Ashbury's basketball team adjusts to the arrival of some new players: girls.

❏ *Courage on the Line* by Cynthia Bates #33
After Amelie changes schools, she must confront difficult former team-mates in an extramural match.

❏ *Free Throw* by Jacqueline Guest #34
Matthew Eagletail must adjust to a new school, a new team and a new father along with five pesky sisters.

❏ *Triple Threat* by Jacqueline Guest #38
Matthew's cyber-pal Free Throw comes to visit, and together they face a bully on the court.

❏ *Queen of the Court* by Michele Martin Bossley #40
What happens when the school's fashion queen winds up on the basket-ball court?

❏ *Shooting Star* by Cynthia Bates #46
Quyen is dealing with a troublesome teammate on her new basketball team, as well as trouble at home. Her parents seem haunted by something that happened in Vietnam.

❏ *Home Court Advantage* by Sandra Diersch #51
Debbie had given up hope of being adopted, until the Lowells came along. Things were looking up, until Debbie is accused of stealing from the team.

❏ *Rebound* by Adrienne Mercer #54
C.J.'s dream in life is to play on the national basketball team. But one day she wakes up in pain and can barely move her joints, much less be a star player.

Ice Hockey

❏ *Two Minutes for Roughing* by Joseph Romain #2
As a new player on a tough Toronto hockey team, Les must fight to fit in.

❏ *Hockey Night in Transcona* by John Danakas #7
Cody Powell gets promoted to the Transcona Sharks' first line, bumping out the coach's son, who's not happy with the change.

❏ *Face Off* by C. A. Forsyth #13
A talented hockey player finds himself competing with his best friend for a spot on a select team.

❏ *Hat Trick* by Jacqueline Guest #20
The only girl on an all-boy hockey team works to earn the captain's respect and her mother's approval.

❏ *Hockey Heroes* by John Danakas #22
A left-winger on the thirteen-year-old Transcona Sharks adjusts to a new best friend and his mom's boyfriend.

❏ *Hockey Heat Wave* by C. A. Forsyth #27
In this sequel to *Face Off*, Zack and Mitch run into trouble when it looks as if only one of them will make the select team at hockey camp.

❏ *Shoot to Score* by Sandra Richmond #31
Playing defense on the B list alongside the coach's mean-spirited son is a tough obstacle for Steven to overcome, but he perseveres and changes his luck.

❏ *Rookie Season* by Jacqueline Guest #42
What happens when a boy wants to join an all-girl hockey team?

❏ *Brothers on Ice* by John Danakas #44
Brothers Dylan and Deke both want to play goal for the same team.

❏ *Rink Rivals* by Jacqueline Guest #49
A move to Calgary finds the Evans twins pitted against each other on the ice, and struggling to help each other out of trouble.

❏ *Power Play* by Michele Martin Bossley #50
An early-season injury causes Zach Thomas to play timidly, and a school bully just makes matters worse. Will a famous hockey player be able to help Zach sort things out?

❏ *Danger Zone* by Michele Martin Bossley #56
When Jason accidentally checks a player from behind, the boy is seriously hurt. Jason is devastated when the boy's parents want him suspended from the league.

❏ *Ice Attack* by Beatrice Vandervelde #58
Alex and Bill used to be an unbeatable combination on the Lakers hockey team. Now that they are enemies, Alex is thinking about quitting.

❏ *Red-Line Blues* by Camilla Reghelini Rivers #59
Lee's hockey coach is only interested in the hotshots on his team. Ordinary players like him spend their time warming the bench.

❏ *Goon Squad* by Michele Martin Bossley #63
Jason knows he shouldn't play dirty, but the coach of his hockey team is telling him otherwise. This book is the exciting follow-up to *Power Play* and *Danger Zone*.

❏ *Ice Dreams* by Beverly Scudamore #65
Twelve-year-old Maya is a talented figure skater, just as her mother was before she died four years ago. Despite pressure from her family to keep skating, Maya tries to pursue her passion for goaltending.

❏ *Interference* by Lorna Schultz Nicholson #68
Josh has finally made it to an elite hockey team, but his undiagnosed type one diabetes is working against him — and getting more serious by the day.

Soccer

❏ *Lizzie's Soccer Showdown* by John Danakas #3
When Lizzie asks why the boys and girls can't play together, she finds herself the new captain of the soccer team.

❏ *Alecia's Challenge* by Sandra Diersch #32
Thirteen-year-old Alecia has to cope with a new school, a new step-father, and friends who have suddenly discovered the opposite sex.

❏ *Shut-Out!* by Camilla Reghelini Rivers #39
David wants to play soccer more than anything, but will the new coach let him?

❏ *Offside!* by Sandra Diersch #43
Alecia has to confront a new girl who drives her teammates crazy.

❏ *Heads Up!* by Dawn Hunter and Karen Hunter #45
Do the Warriors really need a new, hot-shot player who skips practice?

❏ *Off the Wall* by Camilla Reghelini Rivers #52
Lizzie loves indoor soccer, and she's thrilled when her little sister gets into the sport. But when their teams are pitted against each other, Lizzie can only warn her sister to watch out.

❏ *Trapped!* by Michele Martin Bossley #53
There's a thief on Jane's soccer team, and everyone thinks it's her best friend, Ashley. Jane must find the true culprit to save both Ashley and the team's morale.

❏ *Soccer Star!* by Jacqueline Guest #61
Samantha longs to show up Carly, the school's reigning soccer star, but her new interest in theatre is taking up a lot of her time. Can she really do it all?

❏ *Miss Little's Losers* by Robert Rayner #64
The Brunswick Valley School soccer team haven't won a game all season long. When their coach resigns, the only person who will coach them is Miss Little … their former kindergarten teacher!

❏ *Corner Kick* by Bill Swan #66
A fierce rivalry erupts between Michael Strike, captain of both the school soccer and chess teams, and Zahir, a talented newcomer from the Middle East.

❏ *Just for Kicks* by Robert Rayner #69
When their parents begin taking their games too seriously, it's up to the soccer-mad gang from Brunswick Valley School to reclaim the spirit of their sport.